CW00865199

Ways of the West

Ways of the West

Nick Sweet

Copyright (C) 2016 Nick Sweet
Layout design and Copyright (C) 2016 Creativia
Published 2016 by Creativia
Cover art by "matyan90"
This book is a work of fiction. Names, characters, places, and incidents
are the product of the author's imagination or are used fictitiously.
Any resemblance to actual events, locales, or persons, living or dead,
is purely coincidental.
All rights reserved. No part of this book may be reproduced or trans-
mitted in any form or by any means, electronic or mechanical, including photocopying, recording, or by any information storage and
retrieval system, without the author's permission.
nicksweet1@hotmail.com

Chapter 1

Sheriff Bill Hawkins could hear them singing down at the church. The Sheriff was hardly a religious man, but he liked to hear all those voices singing in unison of a Sunday. It gave him the feeling there were lots of good people in the town, all of them with the same idea in their minds.

He'd never been tempted to attend any of the services himself, but he respected those who did. Even if, as had happened today, the noise they made disturbed his slumbers. He liked to think of the good people of Monkford all huddling into the small church, to praise the Lord. Liked to think of them all being happy in their time of worship. Liked to think of them being happy in their faith in the Lord as well as in themselves and their town.

He got up out of bed and shook his head. Still a little groggy from the previous night's drinking, he went over to the sink and splashed some water on his face. He was just putting his trousers on, when the singing stopped abruptly. Something didn't feel right, he thought. Why had it stopped like that?

Hawkins went over to the window and peered out. The sun was already up, and the street was empty of life down below. Something was up: he could feel it in his gut. And whatever it was, he didn't like it.

He finished dressing in a hurry, tied on his gun belt, with his vintage Colt in the holster, and hurried out of the house. His boots raised the dust as he made his way along the main drag. He heard the neighing of a horse as he passed the livery stable. Nothing going on at the bank, as you'd expect on a Sunday. Just then, the batwings of the saloon opened, and Ben Culler came out. Hawkins looked over, and Culler tipped his hat and said, 'Sheriff.'

'Ben,' Sheriff Hawkins said. 'You seen anything happenin' that shouldn't be?

Culler shook his head. 'No, I just been havin' myself a little whiskey, to praise the good Lord in my own quiet way.'

'Seen Steve?'

Culler's bony face creased in a smile. 'Sleeping off what he drunk last night I shouldn't wonder.'

Hawkins didn't have time to go round to Steve's place and get him out of bed. Whatever was happening at the church called for his urgent attention. Sensing there wasn't a moment to lose, he pressed on. As he passed the tailor's, he found himself hoping the singing would start up again. He would have liked to be able to turn around and go back to bed. His head was thumping, on account of last night's Bourbon, and he could really have used another couple of hours to sleep off his hangover.

Then the singing resumed. Only somehow Sheriff Hawkins didn't like the sound of it. It wasn't the singing itself exactly that he didn't like. Hard to say what it was. Just a moment ago, he'd been hoping it would resume so he'd be able to turn around and go back to bed. Only he wasn't about to do that, not now. Now until he'd gone into the church, and checked that everything was as it should be. He wanted to see it with his own eyes.

At that moment, three men emerged from the church. There must have been at least one hundred paces separating the Sheriff and the three men, but they didn't look like God-fearing folk to him. He reckoned he could tell, even at this distance, the sort they were. The no-good sort. The sort he didn't want to see in his town. And if he did see them, then he wanted to hurry up and see the back of them. Only here they were, just having come out of the church, and with the congregation once more booming out the hymn they'd stopped singing earlier.

Every nerve in Hawkins's body told him something wasn't right. Men of this sort didn't attend church. And if they did, then... well, you knew they were up to no good.

A fourth man emerged from the church, and he had a young woman with him. If the Sheriff's eyes weren't deceiving him, it looked like it was the Minister's wife, Kate. She was a fine figure of a woman, and a real good sort, too.

And now here she was, with this no-good looking sort. Only it was clear she hadn't left the church with the man of her own choosing. The shove the man gave her in the back would have set Sheriff Hawkins straight on that score, if he hadn't already been wise to the situation. Then he saw that she had her hands tied behind her back, and that the man had his gun out.

Realizing that he was hopelessly outnumbered, Hawkins knew he had to think fast. It would be no good trying to take the four of them all by himself, here, outside the church. They'd gun him down as easy as a you'd squat a fly. He might be fast enough to take out one or maybe even two of them, but he'd never get all four.

He turned and hurried down to the store, which was at the far end of the street, near to the bank. Got to the door just as John Collins, the man who ran it, was about to close for the day. 'Good idea, John,' Hawkins said. 'Better let me in before you lock up, though. Wouldn't want to turn away one of your best customers, I'm sure.'

The man looked uneasy and put out, but realizing he could hardly turn away the Sheriff, he allowed Hawkins to enter, before locking up for the day. 'Man with a nose for trouble like yours'd make a good sheriff, John.'

'I don't want any trouble.' The storekeeper's eyes were alive with fear.

'No more do I,' Hawkins said. 'But like it or not, trouble's what we got.'

The storekeeper pulled the curtain aside and peered out through the window at the street. 'There they come,' he said. 'They've got a woman with them... it's the Minister's wife.'

Peering out over the head of the diminutive storekeeper, the Sheriff saw the four men coming this way down the main drag, casting shadows before them and taking their time like they had no reason to hurry. The Minister's wife, Kate Sherrin, walked just ahead of them, and whenever she slowed one of them would speed her up with a shove in the back. The men were spread out, and looked like they reckoned they owned the place. Like the town of Monkford was all theirs to do with as they pleased.

Hawkins knew it was up to him to put a stop to what these men were up to; but he couldn't do it single-handed, and he didn't know if he could count on anyone else to lend him a hand. He could sure have done with his Deputy, Steve, being here right now. But he wasn't here, and so Hawkins knew he'd just have to make-do as best he could.

'I wonder what they're going to do?' the storekeeper said.

Without taking his eyes off the four men, as he continued to peer out the window, Hawkins said, 'I'd lay money they're headed for the bank.'

'They're going to rob it, you mean?'

'Shouldn't wonder.'

'And why do you reckon they've got the woman with them?'

'They'll be figuring on using her as a shield if they have to.'

'To stop anyone shooting at them?'

Seeing that Sheriff Hawkins wasn't about to respond, the storekeeper said, 'Don't reckon they're planning on killing her, do you?'

'I hadn't got to thinkin' that far ahead, John.'

'But I bet *they* must have done.'

Once more Hawkins chose not to respond, and the store-keeper said, 'Thought ahead, I mean.'

'What I'm trying to do now.'

'Huh...?'

'Think ahead.'

'Oh.'

Still without taking his eyes off the four men, Sheriff Hawkins said, 'Go and get me your rifle, John.'

'But I don't want any trouble, Sheriff.'

'Little late for that, I'm afraid.'

'Can't we just stay here and wait until this has all passed over.'

'Let those no-goods just go ahead and rob the bank, you mean?'

'There's four of them and only one of you,' John Collins said.

'Yeah, but now I've got you with me that makes two of us.'

'I've never been a fighter, Sheriff. You should know that.'

'There's times when a man don't have no choice, John,' Hawkins said. 'And this is one of them times.'

'But they've got the woman,' the storekeeper said. 'They might use her as a human shield like you said... if you shoot at them, I mean.'

'What'd you propose we do, then, John?' Hawkins asked. 'Just let them no-good sonsofbitches do as they please?'

'Well no, not exactly, but...'

'Good, so go and get your rifle and your gun and any ammunition you've got.'

'How did you know I've got a rifle and a gun?'

'I know everything about this town.'

'How on earth did you get to know so much?'

'I'm the Sheriff here, case you didn't already know it, and it's my place to know things. Now will you stop your whining and hurry up and do as I say.'

The storekeeper sure didn't seem happy about it, but he relented even so, and went and got his Winchester and his Colt.

He looked at the weapons he was holding and said, 'I sure was never planning on using these.'

'Just figured on having 'em about the place as ornaments, that it?'

'Well not exactly, no.'

'Well, then,' Hawkins said. 'Man like you buys himself a rifle and a gun 'cause he knows deep inside him he might need them someday. Ain't that so?'

'Well I guess so, Sheriff... although to tell the truth, I've never really got around to thinking about these things much.'

'Sure you have, John. You think about them every night when you're wrapped up in your bed. You wonder about what would happen if an intruder comes into the house. Then you think about your guns and it kinda reassures you a little. Only then you get to wonderin' whether you'd use 'em or not, don't you? Admit it.'

'Well okay, I suppose thoughts like that have crossed my mind from time to time, Sheriff.'

'And now's that time, John,' Hawkins said. 'The time you hoped would never come, but that you figured surely would come one day.'

'So now what?'

'You can start by loading your weapons.'

'They're already loaded.'

'Good man... that case you're already well prepared.'

The storekeeper's weapons might be so, but a glance at John Collins's face should have been sufficient to tell the Sheriff that the man himself was anything but ready for the situation at hand. But ready or not, he was in it and he was all Sheriff Hawkins had right now by way of a helper, and so the man was going to have to play his part and play it right.

Just then, a man's voice cried, 'Come back here!'

If the Sheriff wasn't mistaken, it was the voice of the Minister he'd just heard. He figured the four desperadoes would have held the congregation at gunpoint and robbed the good people there of everything they had on them. They would have taken any jewellery the women were wearing, and forced the men to hand over their wallets. One of them would probably have grabbed the Minister's wife and tied her hands, and another would have held a gun to her head while the others made their collection round. It was a nasty trick to play on decent, God-fearing folk while they were at church, and it took mean sorts to pull it off. And these four looked about as mean as they come.

Now the Minister was shouting at them, demanding that they let his wife go. 'The Lord will deliver your souls to Hell,' the Minister cried, 'if you persist in your evil-doing.' He was walking up the main drag behind them. The Sheriff figured they must have tied the man up, but that people in the congregation had set him free and now here he was.

The four men carried on walking down the main drag as if they were deaf to the Minister's warnings and entreaties. Without taking his eyes off the scene out in the street, Sheriff Hawkins said, 'Give me the Winchester, John.'

He hefted the rifle, then held it up and sighted along its barrel. 'Go over to the other window,' he said. 'The moment you see me shoot, I need you to start firing, too.'

'But what about the woman?'

'Be sure not to hit her.'

'But I've never been much of a shot.'

'I've got faith in you, John.' Even if that wasn't exactly true, the Sheriff knew that being negative and lacking in confidence never got a man anywhere.

Now the Minster had caught up with the men, and he took his wife by the arm. He acted with a calm and a confidence that seemed oddly out of keeping with the situation. It was as though he thought nothing bad could possibly happen to him or his wife, because they had God on their side. Perhaps he figured the quartet of gunslingers would come to reason, or that he would be able to shame them into giving up their plans to lay siege to the town by appealing to their better nature. Yes, that must be it, the Sheriff found himself thinking. You could see it in the Minister's manner. Confidence of that sort came from a kind of unshakeable inner belief in human goodness. The Minister must be one of those men who believed there was decency in the heart of everyone, and all you had to do was appeal to it.

No sooner had these thoughts crossed the lawman's mind, as he sighted along the barrel of the Winchester, than the four men stopped and turned their attention to the man of God. They seemed to find the Minister amusing, almost as if, instead of being a preacher of the Lord's word, he were a figure of fun, a clown. 'Look what we've got here, boys,' one of them said. 'If it isn't the woman's preacher-husband.'

The Minister went over to his wife and, taking her by the arm, began to lead her back towards church, when one of the gunslingers gave him a push in the back; the Minister's gangly frame lurched forward, and a second man stuck out a leg and tripped him up. The woman went to her husband, as if she were about to help him up; but since her hands were tied, she was unable to do so.

The four gunslingers appeared to find all this rather amusing, and they closed on the Minister's prone figure, forming a gauntlet. He moved onto his side and looked up at the men. 'You will all pay for what you are doing,' he said, 'come the Day of Judgment.'

The men laughed as if they'd just been told a joke. 'The Day of Judgment, huh?' said the tall, slim one. 'And just when'd that be, my friend?'

'When you leave this earth and go to meet your Maker.'

The man laughed, and turned to his companions. 'Hear what the man says,' he said. 'Seems to be concerned for our future welfare.'

'Worryin' about us goin' to meet our Maker,' said the stocky one.

'Well it sure is good of him, don't you reckon?' said the first one. 'To be worryin' about our futures'n all like that...about what's gonna happen to us when we die and go up to meet our Maker.'

'This Maker a yours,' said another of the gunslingers, a man with a big round face and small piggish eyes. 'What sort d'you have him figured for, then?'

'Why it's the good Lord I'm speaking of, you fool,' the Minister replied from where he lay.

'Can't see how this Lord a yours can be so good, seein' as he made the likes of us, is what I'm thinkin'.'

The others laughed.

Even at this distance, Sheriff Hawkins could see the look of horror and confusion on the Minister's face. It was as though he were trying to comprehend how men such as these gunslingers could have been sent onto the earth. Surely, he seemed to be thinking, these men must have goodness in their hearts somewhere, as did other men.

The Minister made to get to his feet, and the gunslinger who was dressed in black made to offer him a hand; but then, just as the Minister pushed himself up off the ground, so the man kicked him hard in the ribs. The Minister cried out in pain, and began to writhe about in the dust like a fish that has been caught on a hook. The others appeared to find all this terribly amusing, and each of them began to kick the poor Minister.

Sheriff Hawkins had been hoping this wouldn't happen. He hadn't wanted to have to try to take them like this. His plan, such as he'd be able to figure one out, had been to allow them to enter the bank, and then send John Collins to go and get Steve, and instruct him to get as many men together as he could and surround the building.

The Sheriff could feel his heart pumping in his ears, as he watched the men through the window. 'You all ready to go when I say, John?' he asked the storekeeper.

'About as ready as I'll ever be.'

'I always knew you'd come good if I needed you.'

The storekeeper made the sign of the cross.

Sheriff Hawkins watched through the window, as the Minister's wife continued in her attempt to come to her husband's aid. She was quite some woman, the Sheriff thought, while wishing that she'd move away in case he was forced to fire his Winchester.

The man in black offered the Minister his hand again, and this time the Minister knew better than to take it. 'You men,' he said through his pain, 'should be ashamed of yourselves for what you're doing here.'

'You're nothing but low, evil scum,' the woman hissed. 'That's all you are... just *scum*.'

'Y'all hear that, boys?' the tall, lean one said. 'The Minister here's wantin' to teach us a lesson and his little missy reckons we're scum.'

The man's companions laughed.

'Any lessons gonna be dealt out round here,' the man went on, 'I reckon we should be the ones to teach 'em.' With that, he aimed another kick to the Minister's ribs, then followed it up with a kick to the man's head. The Minister rolled in the dust, and lay there, inert.

The woman sprang at the man, and one of the others tripped her so that she went sprawling in the dust.

Figuring if he continued to hang fire, the men would pretty soon put an end to the poor Minister, Sheriff Hawkins took aim. He would dearly have liked to get the tall one, but the preacher's wife had just got to her feet and was in the line of fire; so he shot at the man in black. Then all hell broke loose. 'Shoot, John!' he called to the storekeeper, who promptly responded by opening fire on the gunslingers.

I got the one I aimed at in the arm, the Sheriff thought. The man was holding a hand up to the wound as he ran for cover. Hawkins fired at the man again, but missed. The storekeeper was busy firing away, too, but he wasn't much of a shot and kept firing high and wide of the mark.

The men had spread out in no time at all, and now shots were coming into the store through the windows and ricocheting all over the place. The Sheriff knew that he would need to have Lady Luck on his side if he were going to get out of this in one piece. He fired at the stocky one and the man went down, dropping his gun as he fell. The man rolled onto his side and reached for his gun, but before he could get to it he ran out of steam.

Looks like he's a goner, the Sheriff thought. That evened things up a little. There were still three men out there, though, and they were firing in at them for all they were worth.

Two of them were, anyway. He didn't know about the man he'd hit in the arm. He might be out of action for now.

What the Sheriff didn't like, though, was the way the gunslingers had managed to conceal themselves, so that he was unable to see where the shots were coming from. He fired back a couple of times, but then figured he was just wasting ammunition by shooting blind.

He concealed himself and listened a moment; then, when he moved to the side and looked out the window again, a shot whistled past his ear. It had come from over by the livery stable, he thought, seeing a figure move there, and he fired.

The shot must have missed, because the next moment whoever was there fired back. The Sheriff felt a numbing pain and just managed to move to the side of the window, before more bullets came crashing in. He put his hand to the wound. Luckily, the bullet had only grazed the top of his shoulder bone. It was bleeding a fair bit, but he could tell that it wasn't a serious wound.

Just then, the storekeeper fell, and Sheriff Hawkins ducked under the window and crawled on his hands and knees over to him. John Collins was wounded in the chest. 'You're going to be all right,' the Sheriff told him. 'Just hang on in there.'

But the next moment, the storekeeper's eyes closed and his head fell to one side. 'John!' Sheriff Hawkins shook him. 'Don't you run out on me now, you hear!'

He slapped the man's cheek, but there was no response. The storekeeper had breathed his last.

Poor old John, Sheriff Hawkins thought. Always was a peaceful sort, never did want no trouble with nobody. Said so himself. But he stood up when I needed him, and now look at what he got for his trouble. Didn't seem fair, to have John Collins die like this. John was meant to run his store and live to a ripe old age, not get killed in a shootout with gunslingers like this.

The Sheriff's reflections were cut short by another hail of bullets that came in through the windows, sending splinters of glass flying. He crawled over to the window frame, then popped his head up for long enough to get a sight of the gunslinger over by the livery stable and take a shot at him.

He missed again, but then saw something he never expected to see: the Minister's wife, Kate Sherrin, had picked up the gun that was dropped by the man who'd fallen. Then she took aim and fired in the direction of the man who was in the livery. 'Don't, Kate,' Hawkins cried to her. 'You're a sitting duck out there! Come in here!'

Instead of heeding his warning, she fired again. And then her body seemed to go limp, and she dropped the gun and fell to the floor. Sheriff Hawkins was loath to leave the relative safety of the store, and go out into the street, realizing that wouldn't be brave but rather foolhardy. The sight of poor Kate Sherrin lying there in the dust was just too much for him to take, though;

he'd be darned if he was just going to stay there and watch the woman die. If, that is, she wasn't already a goner.

Before he'd given himself a chance to think things through, he struggled to his feet then opened the door and went out into the street. A shot flew past him and hit the wooden frame of the shop. He returned fire, and as he did so the men set off out of the livery on horseback. The man in black made up the rear. He was lying low in the saddle, and the arm that had taken one of the Sheriff's bullets hung loose by his side.

Sheriff Hawkins fired at the men as they rode and they returned fire, but all the shots were wide of the target. He fired twice more, and missed both times, as he made his way over to Kate Sherrin. By the time he fired again, the three gunslingers were already well out of range.

He got down on his knees and felt the woman's neck for a pulse. Nothing doing. She was gone.

Sheriff Hawkins closed her eyelids, then got to his feet. Some Sunday morning it had been.

He walked over to the duckboards, headed on down to the saloon, and went in through the batwings. There was nobody in the place except for Ben Culler. 'The hell is everybody?' he called out. 'Everyone so yella in this darn hole of a town you're happy to leave your fightin' for a woman to do?'

The barkeep, Ray Parsons, appeared from wherever he'd been concealing himself and said, 'Just went to get a new barrel in, Sheriff.'

'That what it was,' Hawkins replied. 'And what about the rest of the men in Monkford? They all so yella they just wanna bury their heads in the sand, that it?'

'You been hit,' Ben Culler said.

'You got that good eyesight, Ben, you'd've come in handy earlier, you'd had a mind to.'

'Never been a match for no gunslingers, me, Sheriff. You know that.'

'You're just a yella drunk, Ben, and you'll always be one… Fact, I feel sorry for ya.'

'No need to insult a man's dignity, Sheriff.'

'What dignity, Ben? You ain't got none of the stuff. Never did have, and never will.' Sheriff Hawkins turned to look at the barkeep. 'Give me some of your best whiskey.'

'You need to have the Doc take a look at that.'

'That I do, Ray. But while I'm waiting for him, I'd be mighty grateful you'd pour me a glass.'

The barkeep poured the drink and set it down on the wooden counter before the Sherriff. He picked up the glass and knocked back the whiskey in a single gulp. 'That stuff does a body good,' he said. 'Give me another, Ray.'

Before he drank this second glass, Sheriff Hawkins yelled: 'If you yella bellies upstairs in those rooms don't hurry up'n get yer asses down here, I'm gonna shoot you all.' With that, he fired a shot at the ceiling.

'But aren't you forgetting you're the Sheriff?' Ray Parsons said. 'You're supposed to be the one who upholds the law in this town.'

'No, I'm not forgetting it, Ray,' Hawkins replied. Then he shouted: 'But I must say I'm getting mighty sick of puttin' my neck on the line for a load of yella livered folk wouldn't cross the street to help me in a moment of need.'

One by one, the doors to the rooms upstairs opened, and men came down to the saloon, accompanied by the women that had been entertaining them. The Sheriff turned his head and looked at the men as they approached the bar. Hank Watts, Bill Pullman, Jerry Smith, Larry Butler. 'Some shower you men are,' he addressed them. 'Where were you a little while ago, when you were needed?'

Fat Larry Butler said, 'You're the one's supposed to uphold the law in this town, Sheriff. That's why you got the badge.'

'That's right, Larry. I do got the badge. But on it's own the badge don't add up to much.'

'Sure it does,' said Jerry Smith. 'It means you're the Sheriff.'

'But a Sheriff's just a man like any other under the badge. He represents the law and maybe he even does his best to uphold it. But he needs the men of the town to stand behind him, if he's gonna have a chance of doing it. And today that didn't happen.' He spat at the floor. 'Today you men all stayed upstairs, out of harm's way, when I needed you.'

'We were sleepin',' Hank Watts said. 'Least I was, anyways.'

'Sure you were, Hank.'

'I was, too,' Bull Pullman protested. He pointed at the Sheriff's wound. 'Look like you been hit.'

'Looks like I have at that.' Sheriff Hawkins drank some of his whiskey. 'It's of interest to any of you, there's a dead body out in the street belongs to a woman. And John Collins got his, too, in the store.'

'You don't say,' said Hank.

'I do say... and you can take that shocked look off your mug, Hank, 'cause it don't wash with the likes of me.'

'Somebody'd better do something.'

'Like diggin' their graves, perhaps you mean?' the Sheriff said. 'Thanks for volunteering Hank. The other men here'll help you do that... but before you set about it, I need somebody to go'n get the Doc.'

'Sure,' Larry Butler said. 'I'll get him to come'n and look at you right away.'

'Tell him there's someone else who needs his attention more than I do, Larry... Or at least, I hope so, anyway.'

'Not sure I follow you, Sheriff.'

'The Minister was lying out in the street, last time I saw him... Not sure if he's still alive or not.'

'Okay, Sheriff, sure... I'll go and get the Doc and tell him to tend to the Minister, and then to come and see to you.'

Larry Butler crossed the bar and went out through the batwings.

'Well, what the blazes're the rest of you men gawping at?'

'Sure, Sheriff,' Hank Watts said. 'Come on, men. Let's get to it.'

Chapter 2

By the time the Doc got to the saloon, Sheriff Hawkins was drinking his fourth glass of medicinal whiskey. The whiskey helped ease the pain from the wound a little, but it still hurt pretty bad. 'Just a scratch,' the Doc said, soon as he'd had the opportunity to look at the wound. 'Expect it hurts like a bastard, though.'

The Doc, an egg-shaped man pushing fifty, who was dressed in a grey suit that he wore with a grey waistcoat and a bow tie, had Sheriff Hawkins sit on a chair and strip down to the waist, there in the saloon. Then he set about cleaning and dressing the wound.

When she saw the Sheriff sitting there like that Molly Gryce, the saloon girl, said, 'Now there's a fine figure of a man, I must say.'

Betty Withers smiled. 'Seems like the Sheriff's been keeping his best qualities a secret from us girls.'

Sheriff Hawkins was in the habit of frequenting the saloon, but he never went upstairs with any of the girls, and so this was the first time any of them had seen him with his shirt off. He'd loved his wife, Moira, dearly, and still missed her as much today as the day when the Lord had taken her, some two years before. And loving her still, and honoring her memory, and the memory of the true and sincere love he'd felt for her – and continued to feel – if, that is, a man can rightly be said to love a woman that's no longer alive – he would be darned if he'd give in to his base and most simple urges, the way a lot of the other men did, and go with the girls of the saloon. Not that he had anything against the girls, as people; he just didn't care to cheapen himself in that way.

'Other patient of mine's in far worse shape, I must say,' said the Doc, who paid scant attention to the saloon girls.

'Way you said that, sounds like the Minister's still alive?'

'Oh he's alive all right, Bill…but he's going to take a while to heal properly. They broke one of his arms for him, as well as some of his ribs and collarbone.'

The Doc finished applying the bandage to the wound. 'There you go,' he said. 'Take it easy for a few days and you'll be fine.'

Sheriff Hawkins had plans for the coming few days, and taking it easy didn't figure in them.

The Sheriff was angry and a man like him can't just sit around and wait for things to pass. He was going after those gunslinging sonsofbitches, and when he found them he'd show them the face of Justice one way or another. He'd bring them in, dead or alive. Problem was, how to find out where they'd gone. He figured going round the neighboring towns would be as good a way to start looking for them as any. So he rode over to Cold Springs, where he called in on his old friend, the lawman there, Harvey Boyle. 'Ain't seen no real trouble here in months,' Boyle told him, as the two men stood at the counter of the saloon on the main drag, talking over a whiskey.

'Oughta touch wood when you say a thing like that, Harve,' Sheriff Hawkins said. 'We had a nasty to-do in Monkford earlier today.'

'You don't say?'

Hawkins described the scene. 'Gunned the Minister's wife down in the street,' he concluded his story. 'No better than if she was a dog.'

'Ever seen them before?'

Sheriff Hawkins shook his head. 'New to these parts.'

'Doesn't give us a lot to go on.'

Just then, a cowboy came in through the batwings and he said hello to Sheriff Boyle. 'How's it going, Joe?'

'Anyone seen the Doc?'

'Shouldn't wonder if he was tending his homestead... Why, has somebody taken poorly?'

The man, Joe, shook his head. 'Guy down at the jailhouse, just ridden over from Fiveways in a frightful panic,' he said. 'Happens three gunslingers rode into the town shortly after sunup. Forced their way into the bank manager's home there'n one of them held his wife and children at gunpoint, while the other two marched the head of the household to the bank and forced him to open the safe.'

Sheriff Hawkins' said, 'Was three of 'em, you said?'

'That's right.'

'So who is it needs the Doc?' Boyle asked.

'Bank manager called the alarm, and they shot him in the leg,' Joe replied. 'Doctor in Fiveways takes the bullet out, tells him to go home'n rest, which he does. Only come the afternoon, the wound's started to infect. Man's in a fever.'

'So why don't they get the doctor in Fiveways to go back and see to him?'

'Turns out old Doc Monks is partial to a drop of the hard stuff. Fallen in the habit of startin' drinking after his meal... which meant he was in no state to ride a horse when they called on him, let along tend to a sick patient.'

'I'd bet my hat those are the three men I was tellin' you about, Harve,' Sheriff Hawkins said.

'Sounds like it, Bill.' Boyle turned his deputy. 'Take a wander out to the Doc's homestead, Joe.'

'Right you are, Harve.' Joe turned and went back out through the batwings.

Sheriff Hawkins said, 'Sounds like they must've come to the region with the plan in mind of hitting a couple of towns and carrying off a pot of money.'

'Maybe we oughter be taking some precautions here in Cold Springs, case they come and try their luck here.'

'Doubt they will, Harve. I got one of 'em with a shot in the arm.'

'That case, I shouldn't wonder if they was to leave the area, go someplace and lie low.'

'Where, though?'

'My best guess'd be west,' Sheriff Boyle said. 'Nothin' there but a wilderness, full of dry desert, rattlers'n lizards... nobody in their right minds is gonna go and look for no gunslingers out there's what they're prob'ly thinkin'.'

'Makes sense,' Hawkins nodded.

'Don't tell me you're goin' after them, Bill?'

'Expect me to sit on my hands and do nothin', Harve?'

'Not exactly, no, but...'

'What, then?'

Sheriff Boyle looked down at his whiskey, then he raised his glass to his lips and drank. 'You're just the Sheriff over at Monkford, Bill,' he said. 'Don't mean to say you gotta goan fight all the townspeople's battles for 'em single-handed.'

'I know that, Harve.'

'So what's all this talk about heading off west after these gunslingers?'

'Won't be doin' it just for the badge, that's for sure,' Sheriff Hawkins said. 'Nor for the townsfolk – most of 'em are nothin' but a bunch a yella bellied bastards, and that's the best I can say of 'em.'

Harvey Boyle set his glass down on the counter. 'What, then, Bill...?'

'You didn't see the woman, Harve... the way she tried to give succor to her husband, after they kicked him – even though they'd tied her hands behind her back... And then the way she took up the dead man's gun and fired at the gunslingers.'

'No, I didn't, Bill.'

'And then the way they shot her down, right there in the street, like she was a dog.'

'I see,' Harvey Boyle said.

Just then, something occurred to Sheriff Hawkins. 'The Doc in this town,' he said. 'I'd like to see him.'

'You mean you want me to take you over to his place?'

'If it's not too much trouble.'

'No trouble at all, Bill... but what's this all about?'

'Got a mind to take a ride over to Fiveways with him, get the lowdown on what happened there from the horse's mouth.'

They rode fast and caught up with Joe, Sheriff Boyle's deputy, on the way to the Doc's homestead, which turned out to be a patch of land some two or three miles outside of town. They found the Doc sitting in the rocking chair in his porch, taking a nap. Sheriff Boyle nudged his arm, to wake him up, and the Doc opened his eyes and looked at him. From his expression, it seemed he scarcely seemed to recognize the Sheriff at first, or know where he was; but he soon recovered his bearings. 'Why, Sheriff,' he said, 'what brings you over here? Don't tell me some-one's poorly?'

'Over in Fiveways,' Sheriff Boyle replied. 'Seems they've had a spot of trouble over there.'

'Have they now?'

Doc Waters, a short portly figure in a grey suit, got up out of his chair and stretched, then reached for his hat, which he'd left on the vacant chair next to the one he'd been sitting in. 'What kind of trouble we talking about?'

'Some gunslingers ran into town and held the bank manager at gunpoint,' Joe said. 'Cut a story short, they ended up shooting him. The Doc there took the bullet out, but he's infected and got a fever.'

'What are they wanting me for?' the Doc asked. 'Haven't they got a doctor of their own over in Fiveways can see to the man?'

'You know Doc Monks has a liking for the bottle.'

'Ah, I see what you mean... that case, I guess we'd better get going.'

The four men mounted their horses and rode over to Fiveways. The land was dry and dusty, with the occasional outcrop of scrub and poverty grass about the closest thing there was in the way of vegetation. Fiveways was about the furthest west you could go before you hit the desert proper. Carry on out there, and all you'd find would be desperadoes and Indians, rattlers and cactus trees.

It took them the best part of half an hour to get there, and they didn't find things quite as they expected. A respectable man, dressed in a pinstripe suit, met them in the street, and he looked mighty pleased to see them. 'Glad you could come, Doc,' he said. 'The sick man's in that house there.'

When they got inside, they saw a man lying out on the table in the living room. A confused look came into Sheriff Boyle's eyes. He knew the manager of the bank in Fiveways, and this wasn't him. 'This isn't Mr. Davis,' he said. 'We were told...'

'No matter what you was told,' said the man on the table. 'Just hurry and get the bullet out of my arm.'

Sheriff Hawkins recognized the man all right: it was the gunslinger he'd shot in Monkford earlier in the day. He reached for his gun. Before he could bring it out of the holster, he felt something hard prod him in the back. 'Hold it right there, mister,' a gravelly voice said. 'One false move and you're dead.'

'Same goes for you two,' said another voice. 'Now the three of you just take your guns out real easy and drop 'em on the floor. Any fast movements and the three of you's dead.'

Sheriff Hawkins realized he had no alternative but to do as the men said. Harvey Boyle and his deputy followed suit. As for the Doc, he wasn't armed. 'That's good,' the man holding the gun against Sheriff Hawkins's back said. 'I can see you men are real sensible and intelligent. Now I want you to kick the guns, so they go under the table.'

The three men did as they told.

'That's it,' the man said. 'Now the three of you goan park your asses on the sofa over there.'

They went and sat on the satin sofa. Then the stocky one gave his gun to the lean, lanky one. 'You three's goan to just sit there and be good,' the lanky one said, 'and we ain't goan have no more trouble, y'all hear?'

Sheriff Hawkins could have kicked himself. He'd smelt a rat no sooner than he'd heard what Joe had to say about the bank manager being shot, and should have known better than to walk into a trap like this.

It was seeing the man welcome them out in the street that had made him think his original suspicious were perhaps wrong; because, contrary to his expectations, the man wasn't one of the three gunslingers. Fact, the man who'd led them inside was dressed in a smart pinstripe suit, with a waistcoat and timepiece, and that had been enough to allay the Sheriff's suspicious, and figure maybe he'd been wrong to suspect the story Joe had told.

No sooner had these thoughts passed through the Sheriff's mind, than the man in the smart suit said, 'When are you going to untie my wife and let us leave?'

'You can just shut your trap and wait,' said the lanky gun-slinger.

'But you've got to play fair. I've done everything you've asked of me, haven't I? Now you've got to let us go.'

'We ain't *got* to do nothin', mister. Now you just shut that gob a yours, you know what's good for you.'

The man's eyes flashed with a mixture of fear and anger, and he lowered his gaze.

So that's it, Sheriff Hawkins thought; they've got the man's wife tied up in one of the other rooms here. These gunslingers were about the lowest form of scum.

And I'm gonna go after them and run these sonsofbitches down, if it's the last thing I do, he promised himself.

The stocky gunslinger came back into the room with some rope, and he commenced to tie up Sheriff Hawkins, along with Sheriff Boyle and Joe. The man tied them all together, so that none of them could move independently.

While this was all going on, the Doc had been tending to his patient. 'It's a deep wound,' he said finally, 'and he's lost a lot of blood...but I'll do what I can.'

'Sure you will, Doc,' the lanky one said. 'You'll save our friend's life, 'cause ya know what'll happen to you if ya don't.'

The stocky one said, 'And not just you either, but there's your friends here, too.'

'Not to mention the girl.'

'What girl?' the Doc asked.

At the same time, the man in the smart suit and waistcoat said, 'You wouldn't kill a woman.'

'Goan be no need for any of that,' the lanky one said. 'Doc here's goan to save our friend, and then we'll be able to take our leave of you nice people.'

The stocky one said, 'Sure you'll miss us when we're gone.'

'No doubtin' that.' The lanky one sniggered.

Question was, Sheriff Hawkins thought, whether the men were just going to leave, if the Doc saved their friend's life, or if they were going to kill everyone first. 'You kill us,' he said, 'and you'll have the cavalry from Fort Bitters after you. They'll hunt you down like dogs.'

'No need to be talkin' so negative, mister,' the stocky one said. 'The Doc saves our friend Earl, then we'll leave here to take a rest until we decide to pay y'all another visit. Ain't that, right, Lee?'

'They ain't goan send no cavalry out to look for us,' said the lanky one, whose name, Sheriff Hawkins now knew, was Lee.

'As things stand, you're right,' Hawkins said. 'But you kill us here then things'll be different.'

The man seemed to be trying to way the situation up. Perhaps he'd already decided to kill everyone in the house, before they left, but now he was having second thoughts. 'We already did some other stuff this mornin'.'

'Did you now?'

'Over in Monkford.' The good news was that the men clearly didn't recognize Sheriff Hawkins, so they didn't know he was responsible for what had happened to their friends – either the one they'd had to leave behind, or the one who was now being tended to by the Doc. Had they known he'd shot them both, then he fancied he would already have been a dead man. He figured he'd better play his cards close to his chest. 'We paid a little visit on the congregation over there when they was havin' their service, made a little collection.'

'That's just robbery,' Sheriff Hawkins said, acting like he didn't know better. 'You won't hang for that.'

'Had to kill one or two on our way out of the town,' the stocky one said. 'Wasn't really meaning to, necessarily... but the minister got to mouthin' off, and that bitch of his wife got involved.'

'You shot the Minister?'

'His wife... was a shootout, and the bitch picked up the gun of a friend of ours that fell.'

Sheriff Hawkins said, 'Killing people in a shootout's one thing, but killing them in cold blood's somethin' else.'

'He's right,' said the man in the smart suit and waistcoat.

'Shut up, both of you,' said the lanky one.

'They'll probably forget about you, if you leave here and disappear into the Territory,' Hawkins said. 'Be more trouble than you're worth for any lawman to go after you... But if you kill us here, they'll have the calvary out after you. You'll never get away.'

'This man's talking a lot of sense,' said the man in the suit.

The lanky man, Lee, turned on him. 'I thought I just told you to shut up!'

'I was only saying that I agree with -'

'Well don't... now shut up the both of you, less you both want me to shoot you dead here an' now.'

They were planning on killing us all, Hawkins thought; but now I reckon I've planted a few seeds of doubt in the man's mind. He knows there's some sense in what I said. Maybe they wouldn't have the calvary out after them, if they shot us all here, he thought; but they'd definitely have a large posse on their tail. And they'd have a big enough price on their heads to have more than one serious bounty hunter go after them.

Sheriff Hawkins could practically see the man reasoning all this out.

The atmosphere changed in the room, so that you could hear the clock ticking up on the wall, as the Doc worked away at trying to get the bullet out of the man's arm. It was hot and you could see the big patches of sweat staining the Doc's shirt under the arms.

Finally, he got the bullet out. 'My,' he said, 'that was a deep one... Now all I've got to do is clean and dress the wound, and he should be all right. Just so long as he gets proper rest.'

'We ain't got time for no rest, Doc.'

The Doc set about cleaning the wound, and then he wrapped a bandage round the man's arm and tied it. 'There,' he said, 'I'm all finished.'

The man in the smart suit said, 'Now you can let my wife Lucy go.'

'Shut up,' the lanky one said. He looked at his friend and said, 'Tie 'em up, Hank.'

With that, the stocky one got busy with the rope.

'But you promised you'd let us go,' said the man in the smart in suit.

'Open that ugly mouth of yours once more, the lanky one said, 'and it'll be the last time you do it.'

The man in the suit looked at the floor, and the gunslinger whose name was Hank tied his hands behind his back. The gunslinger left the room, then came back in shortly afterwards with a woman, who was bound. This, Sheriff Hawkins assumed, must be Lucy, the smart-dressed man's wife. The woman was something of a looker, with her long blonde hair and full bosom. She was trying to say something, or maybe she wanted to scream, but she couldn't because of the gag in her mouth.

Her husband looked at her, and you could see that he wanted to say something to comfort her; but he was too frightened to, after the threat the lanky gunslinger had made a short while ago.

'Okay,' the lanky one said, 'now we're goan have to take our leave of you nice people. And if I might say so, you don't know how lucky y'all are to be gettin' out of this with your lives. But if we ever hear that any of you good folk's had thoughts of testifyin' against us, or goin' to the law, well you might just want to consider the thought that we'll be back. And when we do come back, we'll find the person who welshed on us, and we'll skin him alive and feed his body to the wolves. And if any of you reckon I'm just talkin', then tha's just because you don't know Hank and me, and our friend Earl here.'

Nobody said anything in response to that. Just as well, because if they had then the lanky one would have shot them. Sheriff Hawkins could smell the murdering spirit that came off the man. Only leaving us with our lives because what I said to him earlier set him thinking, the Sheriff thought. He'd as soon kill us all as shoot a rattler. Fact, he was the sort would probably enjoy it.

The one called Hank helped the man Sheriff Hawkins had shot up off the table, and the lanky one, Lee, grabbed the woman. 'You're coming with us.'

'Leave my wife here,' the husband said. 'That's the deal.'

'Ain't no deal.'

'But you said.'

'Sounds to me you ain't understood the situation you're in yet. We're the ones holdin' the guns.'

'But she's my wife.'

'All the same to me who she's married to, mister.'

Sheriff Hawkins said, 'What do you need to take her for? She'll only slow you down.'

'Case any of you folk think it might be a good idea to trail us.'

'But you can't take my wife, do you hear?' the husband said.

'Just watch me.' The man's long face creased in a nasty grin. 'And if any of you cowboys get to thinkin' you wanna play the hero and come after us then you'd better think again. Because if we see anyone comin' after us then the woman gets it, you understand?'

'And what if no one comes after you?' the husband asked.

'Then we'll return her to you in one piece, next time we come by.'

The people in the room listened in silence as the men left the house and mounted their horses outside then rode off. Then everyone in the room began to holler for help, and it wasn't long before people came and untied them.

Sheriff Hawkins was furious with himself for having walked into a trap here, and allowed the three gunslingers to get away from him for a second time. 'I need to go after them, Harve.'

'But you can't,' Sheriff Boyle said; 'not on your own... There's three of them and one of you.'

The woman's husband, John Wilkes, said, 'I'm going with you.'

'But if you'll excuse me for sayin' so, you don't look like no horseman.'

'I don't care, Sheriff. It's my Lucy they've taken, and I'm going after her.'

'Fair enough.'

Sheriff Hawkins said, 'That levels things up a little. And one of them's still recovering from his bullet wound, remember. That'll slow them down a little, till the man's recovered.'

'All right,' Sheriff Boyle said. 'I'm with you.'

'Well, if we're going then the sooner we leave the better.'

'Don't leave without me,' said Sheriff Boyle's Deputy, Joe, as he followed the three men out of the house.

They went into the livery and hired a pack mule, with plenty of water and other provisions; then they mounted their horses and set off out of town. In the distance, they could just see the three gunslingers. This time, Sheriff Hawkins wasn't going to let them get away.

Chapter 3

They followed the trail of the three desperadoes for the rest of the day and didn't stop until after sundown. Sheriff Hawkins had been all for keeping going, but Harvey Boyle reckoned they'd just as likely lose their way in the dark.

They made a fire and cooked some of the steaks they'd brought with them. The steaks tasted good and they opened a bottle of whiskey afterwards.

It soon got cold, and they were grateful for the fire that warmed them as they slept that night. They rose early the following morning and set off once more.

They crossed a large plain, with nothing but patches of scrub and cactus plants and rocky boulders, then they came to a dry gulch. Passing through it, Sheriff Hawkins looked up at the steep rock faces on either side and just hoped there weren't any Indians up there looking down on them. It would be the perfect place for an ambush, he well knew, and the Indians around these parts would know it, too.

All they could hear as they rode along, was the sound of the dry wind passing through the gulch and the hooves of their horses striking the rocky ground. It was an eerie silence, and Sheriff Hawkins didn't like it one bit.

They hadn't got much further before arrows came raining down from above. Seeing Sheriff Boyle fall off his horse,

Hawkins turned and dismounted, then fired a couple of shots, blind, before he grabbed Boyle and pulled him into the shadow of an overhanging clump of rock that served as welcome cover; and John Wilkes followed Sheriff Hawkins and took refuge there alongside him. Unused to violence of any kind, he was shaking and paralysed with fear.

Seeing what had happened, Joe, who'd made up the rear, began to fire in the direction that the arrows were coming from. He was either a good shot or got lucky, because an Indian brave fell from the rock face to his death, landing just a few feet from Joe's horse.

Hawkins turned his attention to Sheriff Boyle. The arrow had got him in the chest. It looked bad. 'You're going to be all right, Harve.'

'Always was a bad liar, Bill.' Harvey Boyle made a brave attempt at a smile, but didn't quite make it; then his head fell back and a fixed stare came into his eyes.

'Harve!' Sheriff Hawkins shook his friend. 'Don't you hold out on me, you hear!'

He felt Boyle's neck for a pulse. Nothing doing.

Something sank in Sheriff Hawkins's chest. He'd always cared for Harvey Boyle. Harve had been made of the right stuff: honest, brave and decent. A man as good as they make them, to Sheriff Hawkins's way of thinking. And now he was gone.

It was my fault, he thought. I should never've got him and Joe mixed up in this. It's my affair and I should've come alone.

But they'd wanted to come, it was true. And Harve was a lawman, besides.

It was a bastard of a thing to happen, though, and Sheriff Hawkins felt terrible.

He would have liked to be able to bury his friend; but there was no way he could do that here.

He glanced over at Joe, who was now looking up at the rock face. Just then, an Indian brave appeared from a crevice in the rock. 'Behind you, Joe!' Hawkins shouted, but too late; because the next moment, the brave flung himself from the shelf of rock, onto the back of Joe's mount. The brave had his knife out ready, and he reached an arm round and tried to cut Joe's throat. Joe was quick to respond, though, and he grabbed the brave's arm. Hawkins took aim but he couldn't draw a bead on the Indian, because Joe kept getting in the line of fire. The two men fell from the horse and landed on the rocky ground with a thump. Hawkins stepped out from under the mass of overhanging rock, and dashed over to where the two men were fighting. The brave was on top of Joe, and he was trying to bring his knife down and cut Joe's throat. Hawkins was about to fire at the brave, when he saw, out of the corner of his eye, another brave who was about to fire an arrow at him from a crevice in the rock face. He turned fast and fired at the brave, got him right in the chest, and the brave fell to his death.

Sheriff Hawkins turned around in time to see the brave who was on top of Joe pushing his knife down, so that the tip of the blade was touching Joe's throat. He fired and got the brave in the head, and the brave collapsed on top of Joe. No sooner had this happened, than an arrow hit the brave in the back, his body serving as a shield to save Joe's life.

Hawkins fired and missed, then fired again and hit the brave that had fired the arrow, and the brave fell to his death. Then another brave appeared through the crevice in the rock face. Hawkins fired at him three times, and missed with all three shots. He fired again, and this time nothing happened. And seeing he was out of ammunition, the brave, who was now only just above Hawkins's head, jumped down on top of him, and before he knew it the Sheriff found himself involved in a life or death struggle.

The brave managed to get on top of Hawkins and was trying to strike him with his tomahawk, but Hawkins had the man by the wrist. They began to wrestle, and Hawkins wondered for a moment if he might have met his match, because the brave was one strong sonofabitch; but then Joe shot the brave, and he fell on top of Hawkins. The Sheriff pushed the brave's body off him, and clambered to his feet. Standing with their guns raised, ready to fire, he and Joe scoured the rocks on either side of the gulch, on the lookout for more braves. They didn't see any.

'Looks like that's all there was,' Joe said. 'We got lucky.'

'We did, but Harve didn't.'

Joe looked at him. 'What you don't mean –'

'Afraid so,' Hawkins said.

Joe dashed over to the body; but then, when he shook Harvey Boyle and realized it was no use, he began to sob. Hawkins patted Joe on the back, and then the Sheriff and John Wilkes lifted Boyle's body up and onto his mount; and Hawkins tied him there, so he couldn't fall off, before they continued on their way. Finally they emerged from the gulch into a broad, dry plain.

'How about if we bury Harve here?' Joe said.

'Good a place as any,' Hawkins agreed.

They dismounted and set about digging the hard soil with their bare hands, for want of a spade. It was hard, unforgiving land anyway, and it was tough going. But they finally dug down deep enough at least to be able to bury Harve in a shallow grave.

'You know anythin' of the Bible, Bill?' Joe asked.

John Wilkes shrugged. 'Never been a religious man.'

'I know a few things,' Hawkins said. 'Not much, but I guess it'll have to do.'

The three men stood by the grave with heads bowed while the Sheriff said the Lord's Prayer. Then he recited the following lines from Isaiah: 'The righteous perish, and no one takes it to heart; the devout are taken away, and no one understands that the righteous are taken away to be spared from evil. Those who walk uprightly enter into peace; they find rest as they lie in death. Amen.'

Deputy Joe and John Wilkes both said, 'Amen.'

Then the men mounted their horses and pressed on across the dry plain. None of them spoke as they rode. Hawkins could see that Joe felt bad about what had happened to Harvey Boyle, and he felt the same way. It didn't seem right somehow that they'd had to bury Harve back there, in a shallow grave in this anonymous plain, far away from his family and loved ones. Old Harve had deserved better than that. But it was the best they could do for him. Sometimes life was like that.

Hawkins supposed the good Lord must have some reason for all the things he made happen, and he knew that good Christians weren't supposed to question God's ways. But even so, he wondered, and he felt downcast and sorry for Harve. And it wasn't just Harve he felt sorry for, either, but for himself, too, and for all the world.

It wasn't right that Sheriff Harvey Boyle had to be killed by an arrow from some Indian brave that didn't even know him. Some savage who didn't know the first thing about the man he'd killed, beyond the color of his skin. It wasn't right that Harve had left a good wife and a little daughter behind, back in Cold Springs, and now both wife and daughter would be forced to face the world without him. It wasn't right that all this had only happened because Harve had come out west on the trail of some no-good sonsofbitches.

Tarnation, it just wasn't right, none of it. And if God was up there looking down, then Hawkins was at a loss as to why He should've let what had happened come to pass.

Why had He even allowed three sonsofbitches like those good-for-nothing gunslingers to carry on as they did, anyway? Why didn't those gunslingers have the spirit of the Lord in their hearts, as other men did?

These and a thousand other questions like them continued to pass through Sheriff Hawkins's mind and torment him, as he and Joe and John Wilkes crossed the broad dry plain.

Chapter 4

The whole town turned out to see Kate Sherrin's body being laid to rest the following morning. The Minister presided over the ceremony, and it was clear to see that it cost him just to stand on his own two feet. Not that he made any kind of complaint; but his suffering was underlined by the slow, almost furtive nature of such movements as he was capable of making, and he would clench his teeth every so often, as he strove to cope with the pain.

Under any other circumstances it would have been only normal to expect the Minister to allow someone else to serve in his place, so that he could relax for such time as he might need to recuperate; but nobody even suggested that he step down on this occasion. It was clear to everyone present that while the man's physical suffering might be considerable, it was far outweighed by the suffering that his heart was being forced to endure.

Nevertheless, the Minister strove with every nerve in his being to rise above the spirit of evil and hatred that had been visited on the town of Monkford by the gunslingers. 'Evil exists in the world,' he told those that were in attendance. 'It would be foolish of any of us to deny as much. Indeed, we saw a terrible manifestation of worldly evil yesterday, here in Monkford, when those three heathens rode into the peaceful haven that together we had striven to create and, in a matter of minutes, destroyed and indeed mocked all our good works.

'Because what happened yesterday, ladies and gentleman, as I hardly think you need me to tell you, was an affront of the most evil kind to every decent impulse that every one of us in this town has ever owned. Those men, possessed as they were by the proud and violent and hateful spirit of Satan, threw down the gauntlet to each and every one of us.

'There are those who have lost loved ones as a result of what happened. I am thinking, of course, of the wife and children of that fine, upstanding citizen John Collins, who ran the store. John was loved by many others, too, as well as his family, and he will be sorely missed.

'And of course I, too, suffered a great personal loss, when my beloved wife, Kate, was taken from me. Such was the love she bore me that Kate tried to comfort me, after I'd been kicked to the ground by the men of Satan, and I cherish her memory all the more for the bravery and purity of her heart.

'Kate was a fine, honest woman, and I am sure that I will not be alone in grieving her loss, along with that of the baby she was expecting. But as Kate's husband and father of the baby that is now dead, I shall grieve harder than anyone.'

At this point, Byron Towers, a robust figure of twenty-five, stepped forward and spoke up. 'I shall miss her, too, Minister, 'cause I loved Kate with all my heart right from the time when we first met in Kansas City.'

'Byron Towers,' the Minister said, 'this is neither the time nor the place for such talk, and if you are truly a gentleman and a man of God then you should know as much.'

Ignoring the Minister as if the man hadn't spoken, Towers looked at the faces of the men present. 'I say we form a posse to go after those three pieces of scum that rode in here yesterday.'

'Tarnation, Byron,' said old John Cox, 'there ain't even no sayin' which way they went. You could be searchin' for them for the rest of your days.'

'I was in Fiveways yesterday,' said Chris Collins, 'and they held Sheriff Hawkins and the Sheriff from Cold Springs and his Deputy captive, along with some other folk, whiles they had the Doc go over there and tend to the man the Sheriff shot.'

'What happened?' asked John Cox.

'The Doc managed to get the bullet out all right, then he cleaned up the wound and the three men left. They took with them Jenny Wilkes, the wife of John Wilkes that works in the bank there,' Chris said. 'Told everyone they'd kill her if anyone came after them.'

'Anyone know which way they was headed?'

'They went west, and right now Sheriff Hawkins, Sheriff Boyle and his Deputy, and John Wilkes, are out there on their trail.'

'But you heard what Chris just said,' the Minister said. 'They said they'd kill that poor woman if anyone goes after them.'

'The poor woman's going to have a fate worse than death if she stays with those three for very long, and that's a fact,' said Chris Collins. 'I'll go with you.'

'Me, too,' said Steve Williams, Sheriff Hawkins's Deputy.

Dan Riley stepped forward. 'Me, too.'

'Okay.' Byron looked at the townsmen. 'Who else wants to come with us?'

The rest of the townsmen who were young enough to join a posse looked at the floor. 'All right,' Byron said finally, 'well if the rest of you folk's too yella then the three of us ain't. At least there's four men in this miserable town that's ready to stand up and be counted.

Chapter 5

The Minister – or Gene Sherrin, to give him his name - went back to his homestead and took to his bed, where he spent the following few days reading the Holy Book. He was in much physical pain, but the pain in his heart was far worse.

As was only natural, he couldn't keep from thinking about Kate. She was one in a million, in his eyes. As he tried to read the Bible, in search of moral and spiritual guidance and succor, so Kate's image would somehow rise up before him, and prevent him from concentrating on the words.

She had the sweetest smile that made your heart turn over when you looked at her. She never even had to say a word - just one look and he knew very well what she meant. It was all there in her smile, those lovely brown eyes of hers that seemed to contain all the warmth in the world. And now she'd been taken from him.

It was written, he well knew, that a man of God was meant to turn the other cheek, and he read this passage through over and over. He was like a man who has fallen out of a canoe in the rapids: things were happening very fast within in, so that he had an awful swirling sensation that was accompanied by feelings of panic and fear.

Gene Sherrin hadn't always been a man of God, and neither had he been instructed in the ways of the Lord as a child. In fact, his father was an outlaw, who'd disappeared after spending a brief sojourn in Kansas City, where he'd met Gene's mother, Nelly, in one of the saloons there. It was an unusual, and indeed some might say inauspicious beginning, perhaps, for a man who sought to learn the ways of the Lord and serve him, but there it was: his mother had been a saloon girl, and his father a gunslinger.

Gene had been brought up in a room in a hotel next to the saloon where his mother worked, and a long string of men served as something like surrogate fathers all through his boyhood. The men would stay with his mother for a while, as his actual father had done, then move on. These men were mostly restless for something they couldn't find; maybe stability was the very thing some of them were looking for, but a regular income was hard to find in Kansas City in those days. So a lot of men were forced to take work when and where they could find it, and when the work dried up they'd move on to the next place.

His mother, Nelly, might have been a common saloon girl, but for him she was all goodness and heart. And although she was clearly not 'respectable', in the eyes of many, he never held that against her; because he knew how much she suffered, and knew also that she only did what she was forced to do in order to keep a roof over their heads.

Whenever he'd been poorly, as a child, she was always there for him, and that was the way things were right up until the day she died. She had been sick those past couple of years, and it was then that she'd made him promise to give up his old ways and try to do some good in the world. By then, Gene had been successful in making enough money to buy a house with a garden for him and his mother, who had long since stopped working as a saloon girl. But her old life caught up with her eventually, even so, in the form of one of the diseases women who live in such a way often ended up with. Syphilis was the word the doctor used. The very sound of it was enough to make Gene Sherrin shudder.

He was there with his mother right to the end, and therefore witnessed the way she suffered, and he suffered right along with her. But even in her suffering, Nelly bade her son read to her from the Holy Book.

'Read me that part again, Gene,' she would say.

'Which part's that, Ma?' he'd ask, even though he knew full well what she meant.

'You know, about Jesus and Mary Magdalene.'

'Ah, that bit,' he'd say, acting surprised, as if he hadn't known all along what she was talking about. 'Okay then, here goes,' and he'd take up the Bible and read in a deep sonorous voice: 'The Twelve were with him, and also some women who had been cured of evil spirits and diseases: Mary Magdalene from whom seven demons had come out – and many others. These women were helping to support them out of their means, and say Jesus cleansed her of seven demons....'

And each time, after he'd finished his reading, Gene would say, 'Maybe if we pray long and hard enough He will do that for you, Ma.'

'Do what, Gene?' she'd say, although she knew very well what he meant.

'You know, the Lord will take mercy on you and cleanse you of your disease.'

'But we mustn't speak that way, Gene.'

'Why mustn't we, Ma?'

'Because I'm not worthy.'

'Why if you aren't worthy, then I don't know who is.'

'People who are deserving.'

'But you're deserving, Ma.'

'No, I'm not.'

'But you've only ever done good in your life – how can you say such a thing?'

'No, Gene, we have to be honest and realistic.'

'What I just said's the truth, Ma... there ain't no person alive's got more goodness in her heart than you.'

'You're only saying it because you're my son,' she said. 'Truth is, I was just a saloon girl, Gene, and there's no getting away from that.'

'You did it because you had no choice... it was either that or starve.'

'Even so, I did things that were wicked in the eyes of the Lord.'

'I'm sure the Lord doesn't see it that way.'

'I slept with all those men, Gene.'

'You slept with them because you needed to eat, Ma.'

'I loved more than one of them, too.'

'There you go, you see.'

'What?'

'You just said that you loved some of them... even then there was love in your heart.'

She laughed. 'I've not been a good mother to you, Gene.'

'You've been the best mother in the world.'

'In that case,' she said, 'why don't you tell me how it was you made the money to buy this house?'

'What's that got to do with anything, Ma?'

'I've got a right to know.'

'I did some business.'

'Rumor is you made yourself a pretty packet from playing poker and working as a bounty hunter.'

'So what if I did? They were bad men I brought in.'

'But the Lord cannot abide violence, Gene,' she said. 'If you would only take up the ways of the Lord, then I should be able to die knowing that I'd at least been a good mother.'

'But I read the Bible to you, Ma, isn't that enough?'

'No, Gene, it isn't... not to atone for the sins we've both committed...' She gazed into his eyes, and he saw in them all of the love in the world. 'I'm not long for this world, son,' she said, 'and if you truly love me as much as you say you do then I'd like you to make me one last promise.'

'Sure, Ma...all you've gotta do is say it.'

'I'd like you to stop living the life you've been living, and become a Minister of the Lord.'

'But you can't be serious, Ma?'

'I've never been more serious about anything in all my life, Gene.' The next moment, after what had been one of the lulls in her illness that enabled her to think and speak with relative clarity, she was overtaken with a bout of coughing that was soon accompanied by the shaking and shivering that were becoming the norm.

'Okay, Ma,' he said. 'I promise... I'll study the Holy Book and then, when I know it well enough, I'll go and see about becoming a Minister someplace where they'll give me a church to preach in.'

Nelly smiled through her pain.

That night she passed away.

Gene was true to his word, and he gave up all of his time from then on to studying the Bible. His studying served a dual purpose, in that, as well as serving to help him on the new path in life that he had chosen, in order to comply with the promise he'd made to his mother, it also helped him find succor in his time of mourning and grief.

After some months of hanging about the house in Kansas City, studying the Holy Bible and grieving for his dear mother, Gene Sherrin entered a seminary, where he studied in earnest for the following two years. Nothing was asked of him with regard to the life he'd lived up until then, and he was not one to give explanations; and so, he was accepted as if he were just another student. His past as a bounty hunter and gambler was well behind him; and now that he was preparing himself for his new life, as a man of the cloth, he would occasionally reflect on his old ways and wonder how on earth he could ever have lived in such a way. Because while it was true that when serving as a bounty hunter, the men he had brought in were for the most part a rotten lot, it was also the case that he was only in it for the money. Serving the cause of Justice had been the last thing he'd cared about. His attitude had been that of a hard-bitten mercenary, so that in many ways he was little different from the men he'd tracked down.

His gambling, too, had only been another facet of this mercenary attitude that he had adopted towards all things in those times. But now he was a changed man, and he vowed that he would never go back to his old ways.

Over time, he came to feel as if his mother were up in heaven, watching down on him, and he became conscious of the importance of acting correctly in all things. And the more he read the Bible in earnest, the more he began to see the essential *rightness* of God's word for its own sake. So that his purpose was now twofold, in that he was not only studying the Good Book to honor his mother's memory, but also to serve God.

Everything had changed in Gene's life, and there was nothing the least bit superficial about this transformation. He came to live his life under the watchful eye of God - at least that is how he viewed things; and he prayed to the Lord several times every day, to ask forgiveness for the sins he'd committed in the life he used to live, and also to thank Him for the joy that He had brought into his heart.

Once he'd finished at the seminary, where his masters were very happy with his progress, he was offered the opportunity of serving at a parish in Kansas City, and he took it without a second thought. He sold the house in Kansas City for a fair price, then packed all his things into a duckboard wagon and rode to Kansas City.

Chapter 6

Byron Towers had never been out West before and so didn't have any idea of the lay of the land. He was a man driven to do what he was doing by his own impulses, and he hadn't really stopped to think things through. Not that he would have been capable of doing so right then if he'd tried, because he was too cut up about what had happened to Kate.

Tarnation if it hadn't been bad enough having her marry that darned Minister and then up sticks and leave with him for Monkford; but he'd always figured he would be able to win her back in the end. Another man might not have shared Byron's unfaltering confidence, especially had they known how deeply and truly Kate had loved her husband – and how deeply and truly Gene Sherrin had loved her right back; but love is blind, as they say, and some of the decisions that a man is liable to make when he is acting under the influence of love can be just as short on insight and vision.

Byron was tall and handsome, and he had a certain gift of the gab and charm so that women had found him attractive. Far from having to run after girls as a young man, he'd had them come after him; or if it wasn't always the case that they'd come right out and given free rein to their impulses where he was concerned, they'd usually found ways, common to the fairer sex, of making their meaning clear enough without having to say a word. Byron had drifted from town to town, working here as a barkeep, there as a stablehand. Kate was working in a saloon when he first met her, so taking her up to one of the rooms had been no great conquest to boast of; but something happened between them that first night, a kind of magic if you will, that conquered both their hearts. Or so Byron felt the following morning, as he lay there naked in the bed, with Kate in his arms, her flesh light and silky against his.

Up till then, when women had fallen for Byron he'd always found himself wondering what they were making such a fuss about; but this time he was the one making all the fuss – or his heart was. Kate was the most special woman in the world, so far as he was concerned; and he only had eyes for her after that.

Six weeks later, she only went and married that darned Minister, didn't she!

Women for you, Byron said to himself, and put it down to a crazy feminine caprice of the sort that a woman can make on the instant and then lament at length. For he was convinced that a woman like Kate could never find happiness – the kind of happiness she'd had with *him* – in the arms of a man like the Minister. She had only married the man, and then run off to Monkford with him, Byron felt sure, to try escape her old life. That was only natural, he reckoned; because Kate had been a clever girl, and so you'd expect her to want to better herself. After all, she was too good to be a saloon girl – any old fool could see that much.

And the Minister had clearly seen it, too.

Byron could have kicked himself for not having asked her to marry him first. She'd have accepted him, he felt sure, and by now they'd have been living happily together as man and wife, and none of this would have happened. (In these reveries of his, Byron conveniently overlooked or forgot the fact that he'd never managed to hold down any single job for more than a few months, and that he was indeed the kind of man who might fairly be described as a drifter.) But he hadn't seen any need to rush things at the time. He'd been able to sleep with Kate more or less when he wanted, almost right up until the day she'd eloped with the Minister – for it had all happened very quickly, and come as a great surprise to Byron - and not only to him but to a whole of other people who'd known the pair, too.

And now Kate was dead and buried, and here was Byron, on the trail of the gunslingers that were responsible for her death. He had yet to come to terms with what had happened, and seemed to be in a semi-delusional state, with part of him grieving for Kate, as another part of him somehow managed to continue to yearn for her, almost as if reckoned he could still win her back.

As for Dan Riley, he was a thickset man of twenty-four, whose bitter cast of mind owed something perhaps to his own temperament but also much to his having lost his young wife, Ruby, the year before to typhus. Ruby had been expecting their first born, and the child had died with her. Since then, Riley had become more taciturn than ever, and it was as if he blamed some evil spirit he reckoned to be at the root of all things for his great loss.

Dan Riley had been out of town when it all happened, and had arrived after sundown to find the townsfolk in mourning. He instantly felt as if the 'Evil spirit' that had taken Ruby and their first-born had come back to haunt Monkford, in the form of the sonsofbitches who were responsible for the deaths of Kate Sherrin and John Collins, and he lamented the fact that he had not been present when the shooting took place, so that he could have stood up to the gunslingers.

Reading between the lines, as he listened to the townsfolk tell what had happened, while he drank whiskey at the counter in the saloon in Monkford, Dan Riley suspected that a great number of his fellow townsfolk – the vast majority, in fact – had shown themselves to be yellow bellied cowards when the shooting started. Sheriff Hawkins had stood up to them all right. So had the storekeeper, John Collins, and he'd paid for doing so with his life.

What affected Dan Riley most of all, was the story of what happened to the Minister and his wife. Riley had taken to attending church of a Sunday, ever since he'd lost his wife; and he'd found a kind of solace in the words of the Holy Book, as delivered by the Minister, Gene Sherrin. Up until the time of his loss, Dan had never been a regular churchgoer, and had never really given much thought to religion; but in his grief, he found succor in God's word.

It was hardly surprising, then, that Dan had come to feel a sincere respect and even fond affection for the Minister, who was after all the good Lord's representative here, in Monkford. He was grateful to the man for bringing the word of God into his life, just at the time when he was most in need of it; because he'd feared what might happen to him, had he been left to try to mourn his loss alone.

And when he saw the Minister's wife with him at church of a Sunday, Dan Riley reckoned they were the most wonderful couple he'd ever come across, and just the finest people he knew; and it was as though the affection and respect he felt for the Minister spread to the man's wife. He didn't feel possessive in any way about Kate Sherrin, you understand; no, he was quite unlike Byron Towers in this regard – his feeling for the Minister's wife was purely Platonic, and based on a healthy respect.

When he heard of the way the Minister had been kicked around in the street by the gunslingers, and then how the man's wife had been shot down like a dog, something rose up in Dan Riley's heart. He was no gunslinger; in fact, he was a simple farmer. But he was of stout heart and firm faith, and was determined to bring the heathens who had visited Hell upon Monkford to justice.

As for Chris Collins, he was a slightly headstrong young man of twenty-one, who fancied himself with a gun, even though he'd never done much to warrant his idea of his own powers. Chris had been scared at the time, when the gunslingers came into town, and had done nothing; and afterwards, he'd hated himself for his passivity and cowardice. Then when he learned that his favorite uncle, John Collins, whom Chris always loved but somehow suspected of being a timid and cowardly man, had taken up arms against the gunslingers and paid for it with his life, Chris's self-hatred grew to unmanageable proportions. He didn't know how he'd ever be able to live with himself, if he didn't do something to put things right. Why, he told himself, if those sonsofbitches ever rode into Monkford again then they'd find out... But of course, there was nothing to say that the men ever would return. They might; but then again, they might not.

Chris passed the night grieving over his beloved uncle and hating himself for his own failure to stand up and be counted, and he shed tears of grief and rage at John Collins's funeral, which took place at ten-thirty the following morning. By the time Kate Sherrin was buried, directly afterwards, Chris was in a rare state of emotion. Then when Byron Towers challenged the men present to go after the gunslingers with him, Chris new that he had to step up.

As for Steve Williams, he was Sheriff Hawkins's Deputy, and if the Sheriff was out there on the trail of those three no-good sonsofbitches then he'd be darned if he would be left behind.

And so here there were, the four men who made up the posse that left Monkford on the trail of the gunslingers: Byron Towers, Dan Riley, Chris Collins and Steve Williams. Considered in the cold light of day, they were an enamored and semi-delusional drifter, a bereaved farmer, a young man who'd felt shamed into joining the posse by the knowledge of his own cowardice, and Sheriff Hawkins's Deputy. Only one of the four men – Deputy Steve Williams – could claim to have any real experience of expertise with firearms. Some posse! But here they were, trailing three of the meanest and deadliest sonsobitches this side of Hell into the Territory.

Chapter 7

When Gene Sherrin became a Minister in Kansas City, he felt a calm in his heart and mind the like of which he'd never known before, or at least not since his childhood. He was living, he felt, in the peace that was the due of those who served the Lord. Nevertheless, there were times when he felt lonely and in need of a mate, since he was a man just like any other – his having become a man of the cloth had changed nothing in that sense.

A number of women made a show of interest in him, among his parishioners; all of them staid, sensible women who sought to follow the teachings of the Holy Book – or so he believed, even if the truth was some of them only attended church to seek a mate or position themselves at the fount of all the gossip that did the rounds. But Gene managed to survive or deflect the advances of the women who set out to flirt with him and court his favor – until, that is, Kate Connolly (as she was then) began to attend mass every Sunday. There was something different about her, he thought. She wasn't one of these staid matronly sorts who wished to run his house for him and thereby find themselves the object of envy of so many of the other ladies in the vicinity. No, this young woman seemed to attend church for quite a different purpose. Quite what that purpose was, Gene wasn't sure at first; but he was determined to find out.

Every time he stood in the pulpit of a Sunday and gazed out upon his congregation, he would notice the rapt expression on her pretty face that lent her the appearance of someone who is lost in a world of her own.

As the weeks wore on, so Gene found himself looking for the woman's face; and when he spotted her sitting there, in her usual place (on the end of the fourth row back, next to the aisle), something would leap up inside him. He wondered if he were falling in love with this woman. How absurd, he scoffed at his own thoughts. A man in my position, falling in love with some woman just because she has a pretty face, just like some school-boy! Absurd or not, though, he continued to wonder about her, and to keep an eye out for her face each Sunday, before beginning his sermon.

Who was this woman? he wondered. And was she married?

Very possibly, he thought.

And yet, there was something about her, something about her solitary manner, and the rapt *expression* that would come into her face, as she sat there in her pew, among the congregation each Sunday, that caused Gene Sherrin to wonder. Somehow, she just *looked* like she was single. He couldn't have said why he felt this, but he did. Call it intuition, if you like.

Then one Sunday, he climbed up into the pulpit and gazed out at the faces of the members of his congregation, before starting on his sermon, the same as every week; only this week something was different. He didn't know why this was so, exactly; but he could *feel* it in his bones. A sort of panic ran through him, as he scoured the sea of faces before him with his eyes; and now he realized what it was: indeed, something truly *was* different this week – the face of the girl he'd come to think of as the Mystery Woman was nowhere to be seen.

Where was she? he wondered. Why hadn't she come to church this Sunday? His blood raced through his veins, and his legs went a little weak, even if he would have been loath to confess as much, even to himself, proud as he was.

Of course there were lots of possible explanations for the woman's absence from the congregation, none of which he was in a position right then either to confirm the veracity of or discount. Even so, he found himself considering a number of possible eventualities, as he opened the Holy Bible and turned the pages. Perhaps she's not feeling very well, he thought. Yes, that was the most likely explanation.

She would almost certainly be back in her usual place again next Sunday, he told himself. But what if she wasn't? What if she'd left Kansas altogether?

The mere thought of this was sufficient to cause Minister Gene Sherrin's head to spin. I really am a fool, he thought; and he told himself that he must get a grip. The people were waiting for him to begin his sermon, and here he was bothering about things that in truth were none of his business.

He began to read from the Bible. This week he had chosen to tell the story of the Good Samaritan. The passage had a pleasing, homiletic quality to it, he felt; and yet he found himself reading it today without paying much heed to the words of the Holy text, even as he uttered them.

The rest of the service went the same way. Somehow, he got through it all without really giving much thought either to his own words, or the reactions of the people in his congregation. Given the great enthusiasm he felt for his calling, this just wasn't like him.

What was wrong with me today? he asked himelf afterwards, when everyone had left. But he knew very well what it was. *She* hadn't come to church to day, and he'd missed her.

Seems like I really am in love with the woman, he thought.

He waited for the following Sunday to come round with an impatience that he had not known in years, and which, had he taken greater heed of his reading of the Holy Book, he should have known ran against the grain in so far as the good Lord's teachings were concerned. But he was a man divided: he was still the preacher, with his faith in God intact – that hadn't changed; yet now there was another facet to his personality, and this new part of him was in love. At least, that is the way he came to understand his predicament, or explain it to himself; and, indeed, seek to make sense of it all, he did, for he was much given to self-analysis, a trait that was perhaps as much part of his character as it was a habit of thought he had picked up during his time in the seminary.

So he waited for the following Sunday to come round; but when it did, once again there was no sign of the woman.

He made discreet enquiries among some of the parishioners, always taking care to talk as if his interest in the woman were solely that of a Minister concerned for the well being of his congregation, and not that of a man so enamored as to be close to the end of his tether. And it turned out that the widow Jane Bowen knew of the woman. 'She's nothing but a shameless hussy that one, Minister,' she assured him. 'Been coming here all dressed up to the nines every Sunday, like she's somebody respectable, a veritable pillar of the community, when all along it turns out she had us fooled – or she thought she did... But she didn't bargain on Mary Thorndike's talent for digging out gossip.' Jane Bowen's upper lip rose in a grin that had far more cruel disdain and contempt than charity about it. 'Transpires her name's Kate Bloom,' the widow went on. 'Her folks emigrated to escape the potato famine in Ireland, then foundered over here just as they had in their country of birth. As a girl, she was more or less left to bring herself up, and has been working in one of the saloons down town ever since she was old enough to -'

'Which saloon would that be?' the Minister interrupted her.

'Well Minister, now there's a strange question to ask,' Jane Bowen replied. 'Knowing me as you do, I hardly should've thought you'd be expecting me to know anything about what goes on in the saloons in this city.'

'No, quite, Mrs Bowen.' Gene Sherrin tipped his hat, figuring anything he might add was only likely to see him digging himself into an even bigger hole in the ground where the widow was concerned; and with that, he turned and took his leave of her.

At least he had learned what he'd wanted to know. Although in truth, he was more than a little surprised to find out that the woman he was so enamored of turned out to be a saloon girl. He recalled that his own mother had been forced to adopt the same lifestyle, and so, far from causing him to lose interest in the woman, what he'd discovered only seemed to increase his interest in her.

Nevertheless, there was another side to all this; because he was well aware that his congregation had certain expectations about the kind of man they wanted for a Minister in their parish, and he was quite sure that courting the favors of a saloon girl was not the kind of behavior that would be likely to win him a place in many people's good books. It would be necessary to proceed with caution, he realized, if he didn't want to make a pig's ear of everything he had worked so far to achieve.

He pondered the situation for a while, and decided that, since the good Lord loved all of His subjects, and perhaps the black sheep of the flock most of all, he might quite reasonably justify going in search of a saloon girl in his capacity as Minister.

His mind made up, he rode into town the following morning, and began to make enquiries in the saloons. There was a woman by the name of Kate in the first place he visited, but the barkeep said he didn't know the woman's surname. He asked the Minister if he'd liked to speak to the woman in question, and Gene Sherrin nodded and said he would; so the man went off and came back minutes later with the girl, having got her down from one of the rooms upstairs. She was a buxom brunette, pale and with freckles on her cheeks. 'No,' the Minister said, 'this isn't the woman I'm looking for.'

'What's it all about?' the girl asked.

'I'm looking for a woman by the name of Kate Bloom.'

'I'm Kate Taylor, mister... but I think I know the girl you mean.'

'Do you know where I can find her?'

'Try Dixon's.'

'And where'd that be?'

'Turn left when you leave here, then it's the second on the right.'

The Minister thanked the girl and went on his way; and he soon found the place. He entered and went up to the counter. The barkeep came over and eyed him a little suspiciously: it was the look a barkeep gives someone who clearly hasn't set foot in a saloon in a long time. 'What can I do for you, mister?' the man asked.

'I'm looking for a woman.'

The barkeep smiled. 'Well we got plenty of them here...'

'No,' Gene Sherrin hastened to add, 'a particular woman, I mean...'

'This woman got a name?'

'Kate Bloom.'

'That case,' the man said, 'you've come to the right place... Like me to go and get her for you?'

'I'd appreciate it if you would.'

The barkeep went upstairs and reappeared shortly afterwards. 'Just woken her up,' he said. 'She'll be down in a minute.'

'Thanks.'

'Can I get you anything while you wait?'

'No, I'm fine thank you.'

Gene Sherrin took a seat sat at one of the tables. There were a couple of men standing at the counter, drinking whiskey, but the place was otherwise empty.

The woman came down dressed in a long blue dress. Her face was pale and her eyes, which were puffy from sleep, opened wide when she saw who it was that had come calling on her. 'Why hello,' she said. 'But you're the Minister, aren't you?'

'Yes, that's right.' He had already risen from his chair and was fingering the rim of his hat in a nervous fashion. 'I hope you don't mind my calling on you like this?'

'No, not at all.' A cautious expression came into her face. 'But what is it that brings you here?'

He ventured a smile. 'Perhaps you'd like something to drink?'

'I wouldn't say no to a coffee,' she said in a stage whisper, and looked over at the barkeep.

The Minister pulled out a chair for her and she sat on it. She patted at her hair with her hand. 'I was sleeping,' she said. 'We don't usually get callers of a morning.'

'I saw you at church,' he said. 'But you've not attended these last two Sundays.'

'I've been busy.' She looked away, and then when she turned her head to face him there was a puzzled expression on her face. 'You noticed me, then?'

'Yes.'

The barkeep came over and put Kate Bloom's coffee down on the table before her, then he looked at Gene Sherrin. 'Sure I can't get you somethin'?'

He shook his head, and the barkeep went back behind the counter.

Kate Bloom sipped her coffee. 'So,' she said, 'you saw me in church...?'

'Yes... but you've stayed away these past two Sundays.'

She nodded. 'I told you, I've been busy... What of it?'

'I wondered what had happened to you,' he said. 'If perhaps you were poorly or...' He began to play with the rim of his hat.

'Or *what* exactly?'

He shrugged. 'Well that's just it – I really had no idea…' He smiled. 'That's why I thought I'd come and look you up.'

'To make sure I'm okay?'

'Yes.'

'Well now you've found me,' she said. 'What do you think – am I okay or not?'

He laughed. 'You seem to be, so far if I can tell.'

'If looks don't deceive, you mean?'

'I suppose that's what I mean, yes.'

'But they do, Minister…that's one thing I can tell you.'

He was confused. 'Is something the matter, then?'

'Yes and no.' She sipped her coffee. 'How did you find me, anyhow?'

'One of the women in the congregation told me I might be able to find you here.'

'Did she now?' Her face creased in a rather odd smile. 'That was mighty kind of her, I must say.'

'As Minister of the parish,' he said, 'I feel it is incumbent on me to take an interest in my congregation – just as a shepherd must take care of his flock.'

'Truth is, Minister,' she said, 'I used to like to go to church. It made me feel like I could escape from this place and the life I live here for an hour or two…I'd do myself up to look all respectable, like I was one of these mighty fine ladies whose husbands work in a bank or someplace important and lives in a nice house with a garden, and maybe has a little land…' She looked at him and there was a strange, almost furtive expression in her eyes. 'You get the picture, anyway.'

'Sorry,' he said, 'I'm afraid I don't quite follow you.'

'I wanted to pretend, even if it was just for an hour or two each Sunday, that I was really somebody…instead of being who I am.'

'And what's wrong with just being yourself?'

'Look at me,' she said. 'What do you see?'

What he saw was an attractive young woman who made his head spin, but he could hardly tell her that.

'You're not saying because you're too polite,' she said. 'But I'll tell you...you see a common saloon girl who earns her daily crust by consorting with the dregs.'

'The good Lord doesn't judge people in that way.'

'It's pretty to think like that, isn't it?'

'It's not just a pretty thought,' Gene Sherrin said. 'It's the way the Lord works...to Him we're all the same.'

'You mean to say He doesn't judge us?'

'Oh, He will do that all right, come Judgment Day...but he doesn't judge us in the way you mean, Miss Bloom.'

'You know my surname.'

'Of course...I would have had a difficult job finding you if I didn't.'

'What else do you know about me?'

He shrugged. 'Nothing, I'm afraid...beyond the fact that you work here and that you've been to church a few times, and then you stopped coming.'

She gazed at him as if he were something most unusual. 'Do you go to this trouble for all your parishioners, Minister?'

'I try to...'

'But there must be others that've attended services a few times then stopped going,' she said. 'Perhaps they left town or just lost interest...isn't that so?'

'Yes, that's true I suppose.'

'Did you go running round Kansas looking for them, too?'

He blushed. 'My my,' she said. 'I do declare that you've gone red.'

Gene Sherrin had feared that something of this sort might happen. He'd tried to steel himself against making a demonstration of his feelings, but it seemed that the heart had a tongue and the more you tried to silence it the more it liked to talk. 'I really must be getting along,' he said.

'There's nothing to be ashamed of, you know.'

'I'm sorry?'

'You wouldn't be the first man of the cloth to fall for a woman's charms – even if it is a saloon girl, like me.'

'Aren't you rather jumping the gun, Miss Bloom?'

She grinned, and he would dearly have loved to take her in his arms and plant a kiss on the curve of her painted red lips; but he did not dare. 'So you were worried that I might be poorly...?'

'Yes, or in some kind of trouble...'

'And if I was in trouble of some sort, what were you planning to do about it?'

'I thought perhaps you might need some help.'

'Help...?'

'Yes.'

'Just how would a man like you set about helping a woman like me?'

'Through the power of prayer, Miss Bloom,' he said. 'What else?'

He got up from his chair. 'Anyway, I really must be getting along.'

'Okay,' she said, 'well thanks for coming in to see me, Minister... it was a pleasure.'

'I hope to see you at church on Sunday.'

'I'm not sure that would be a good idea.'

'Why on earth do you say that?'

'Some of your parishioners hardly approve of me, Minister,' she said. 'They've found out about me, you see.'

'Found out...?'

'That I work here, as a saloon girl.' She sighed. 'I thought if I dressed up smart, and what with the church being the other end of town... well, I thought I might get away with it.'

'You talk as if you were robbing a bank or something.'

She smiled. 'That's almost the way I felt about it... yes, like I was tricking people, or trying to... But some of your parishioners saw through me, and they found out. I can hardly go back there now.'

'But why can't you?'

'Don't you see?' There was a sort of awe in her eyes as she gazed at him. 'They know I'm a saloon girl, and they disapprove of me... Far as they're concerned, I'm not welcome in that church of yours. They think I'm scum.'

'I doubt that, Miss Bloom.'

'They told me so to my face,' she said, '- said they'd be happier if I didn't show my face in the congregation ever again.'

'Who said this?'

She shrugged. 'I don't know their names - two old bats that go there.'

'Well they should be ashamed of themselves.'

'When they spoke to me in that way, and said those things,' she said. '...Well, *they* didn't look like they were ashamed of themselves at all; but that's how *I* felt.'

'But why would you feel that way?'

'I guess because they felt they had the right to talk to me as they did.' She thought about what she'd just said. 'I suppose I thought I really must *be* worthless, if those ladies, who were done up in such expensive clothes, reckoned they could say such things to me.'

'Well those ladies are wrong, and I've a good mind to confront them and point out the error of their ways.'

'Oh don't do that, please.' She placed her hand on his sleeve. 'You'd only make me feel worse if you did.'

He sighed. 'I should very much like it if you would come to the service on Sunday,' he said. 'And if anyone says so much as a word to you that isn't kind or polite, then I'd appreciate it if you would let me know and I'll make my feelings known to them... My church is the house of the Lord, and I just won't tolerate nastiness of the sort you've just described taking place in it.'

'You're a very kind man.'

'It's got nothing whatsoever to do with kindness.'

'What has it got to do with, then?'

He looked at her. 'Promise me that you'll come on Sunday.'

'Okay,' she said. 'I'll go… even if it's only to keep you happy.'

'Now you've promised – so if you don't come you'll be breaking your word.' He put his hat on and tipped it. 'Good day to you, Miss Bloom.'

Chapter 8

Come Sunday, the woman Gene Sherrin had spent so much time thinking and, yes, even fantasizing about, was there in her usual place in the congregation. He felt a warm feeling of joy spread through his entire being that he knew had nothing to do with the word of the Lord. Or perhaps it did, though. After all, was love not what God was all about?

He'd chosen the story of Jesus and Mary Magdalene for his sermon, and he delivered it in a defiant tone and manner. It was as if he felt the need to atone for some misdeed. At the same time, he told himself that he'd done nothing wrong. What if he was in love with Kate Bloom? And what if she was a saloon girl? Was there anything wrong in any of this? If there was then he'd like to have someone point out the place in the Holy Bible where it said it.

He justified his thoughts and emotions to himself in this way, and his mood of defiance and indignation came close to anger, so that he finished the sermon in what sounded like a storm of rhetoric. If his congregation were all passengers on God's ship, then the Minister's words were a storm that had been visited on said craft. And it wasn't just his words, and the way in which he bellowed them out, as if he were delivering them in the form of a challenge to his parishioners, that were unusual today; for the look in his eyes and the expression on his face appeared to indicate that he was not only aware of and affected by the ravages of the tempest, but that the tempest was doing its worst work within his very heart. He had the fanatical appearance of a man who is at war with himself; a man who is suffering the ravages of a deadly passion. It was still not too late, he realized, for him simply to turn his back on the storm. There was nothing forcing him to go forth into the very heart of it. No, he might, if he so wished, simply carry on about his daily life as he always had. The fact that Kate Bloom had kept her promise and come to attend church today did not of itself place any obligation on the Minister. He might simply smile at the woman, and that would be enough. Or, if she made a point of seeking him out to talk, then he might simply congratulate her on having made the right choice in coming to church; and he might even say that he was glad to see her, and still, having said that much, he might reasonably be able to claim that he had done nothing amiss.

But then how would he continue about his life as if nothing had happened, if his heart were in a state of perpetual torment? That was the question. He was, he told himself, a man like any other; even if he was God's representative on earth in his parish, he still had the right to take a wife. After all, it was not the Roman Catholic Church to which he had sworn his allegiance.

He supposed it was the woman's being a saloon girl that would shock people. His congregation would not stand for that, he felt sure.

The sermon finished, he asked the congregation to stand and led them in singing the Lord's Prayer, and once more his voice was charged with the tones of an angry and almost menacing passion as he bellowed out the words. Anyone who observed him closely might have been forgiven for thinking that here was a man on the brink of committing some rash and perhaps even violent action. The Minister was conscious of the passion that raged within him, and yet it was as if he were powerless to fight against it. And then there was the little voice inside it head that kept saying, But why *should* I fight against it? Why *shouldn't* I love Kate Bloom? If she'll have me, then *why shouldn't* I take a former saloon girl for a wife?

Things were moving very past inside of him, because here he was considering the whole business of marrying the woman. The fact that he scarcely really knew her seemed hardly to be of concern to him. That was because somehow he sensed that he *did* know her, on some subliminal level. He felt that he could tell exactly the sort of woman she was, and that she had a good heart and would make him an excellent wife. Quite how he reckoned he could know all this about Kate Bloom, just from having seen her face among many at church on a Sunday, and after having spoken to her just the one time when he went to visit her at her place of work, may strike some people as an interesting ques-tion. But Gene Sherrin might well be a church Minister, yet he was also a man; and he'd been a man for some time before the notion of becoming a preacher had ever entered his head; and during that time, he'd known a fair few women. And having known women as he had, he reckoned he'd come to develop something of an eye for them; not just in the sense of whether they were pretty or not to look at, but of what they were like as people. And he reckoned, just from looking at her the times she'd come to church, and from the time he'd spoken to her – brief as their intercourse had been – that he knew the kind of woman he'd come across in Kate Bloom. She'd make any man an excellent wife, he felt sure of it. All right, she might be a saloon girl, but she'd told him that she didn't like the life she had fallen into and, were she given an opportunity to leave it once and for all, he felt sure that she would do so without a second thought; and that having done so, she would be only to happy to leave her old ways – the need to sleep with different men – behind as well. For she was not, he reckoned he could tell, one of those women who like to sleep around because they are made that way; no, she only did it because she'd fallen on hard times and was faced with no alternative: a young woman in her position, with no family to fall back on, either had to ply to the whims and desires of the men who frequented the saloon or find herself without a roof over her head and with no means of supporting herself.

All these thoughts kept running through the Minister's mind, over and over, as he led the congregation in the Lord's Prayer; and his eyes had a wild glare in them, which only softened into a mild gaze when he happened to make eye contact with Kate Bloom. Had he considered matters a little more fully and honestly, then it might have occurred to him that while he had made great strides in studying at the seminary to become a man of the cloth, he was nevertheless a man with a past; and that past, whether he liked it or not, was still a part of the man, Gene Sherrin, even if the Minister strove to deny its existence. Just as the leopard in the famous axiom never changes his spots, not because he doesn't wish to but because he *isn't made that way*, so Gene Sherrin was a man who'd always needed a certain kind of woman in his life. He might have hidden this need for a while - hidden it, indeed, even from himself – but now he found himself face to face with the woman who embodied all or most of the qualities the masculine side of his nature, deep down inside him, required in a mate, that part of him reared up and revealed itself, and even had the Minister wanted it to go back to where it had come from, Gene Sherrin, the man, was powerless to wish for this simply because he was incapable of being anything other than himself.

He led the congregation in a final hymn, his voice booming out the words of *Onward Christian Soldiers* as if it came up from the very bellows of the earth; and then all that remained for him to do was remind his listeners to go about their lives in a way that would please God, and he bade them all good day. With that, the parishioners began to make their way out into the aisles and then they moved into a slow column towards the doors; and watching them, Gene Sherrin's heart pounded in his chest, as his eyes roamed over the sea of bodies before him, in search of the woman who had stolen his heart. There she was: instead of leaving her pew and making her way out of the church, along with the others, she had chosen to sit down, perhaps to wait until everyone else had gone.

Perhaps she expects me to go over and talk to her, Gene Sherrin thought, while the Minister in him flushed at the prospect of an encounter with the woman. He could scarcely go to her right now, anyway, with all of the parishioners blocking the aisles; so he pretended not to notice her sitting there, and busied him by turning the pages of the Bible on the lectern, as if he were searching for a particular passage. In actual fact, the words of the Holy text swam before his eyes, whenever he stopped turning the pages and, in an attempt to give the impression he was trying to find out if *this* was the passage he was looking for, set about reading a few lines.

He passed a long few minutes in this way, and when he finally looked up, the hubbub of chatter that the parishioners made as they left the church having stopped, he saw that the building was now empty, with the single exception of the woman who was still sitting in her pew. He realized that the moment of truth had arrived. For just as soldiers find their moment of truth arrives in battle, when they find that their lives are on the line and everything can be won or lost in the beating of an eyelid, the same is true of lovers. He could go over to the woman and make a profession of his feelings for her, or he could do nothing. Alternatively, he could go over and speak politely to her, but in his capacity as a Minister, and in that way the moment might also pass without event.

The man and the Minister were at war within him, as he stepped down from the pulpit and went over to where she was sitting. 'I'm glad to see you kept your promise, Miss Bloom,' he said and smiled.

'How could I not, Father, when you went out of your way like that to find me and ask me to come?'

'But you didn't just do it for me.'

She got to her feet and gazed into his eyes. 'You're a mighty persuasive man,' she said. 'It's like you're a preacher and yet you're not.'

'What do you mean by that?'

'I don't rightly know.' It was an intuition of hers; something she couldn't have explained if she'd tried. 'You're not like any Minister I've come across before.'

'Come across a number of them, have you?'

'I've been to a few other churches in my time,' she replied. 'I never had what you'd call a proper home as a girl, and sometimes coming to church gave me a sense of what I was missing, you know?'

'It seemed like home to you?'

'Yes, in a way.'

'Every church is God's home.'

'I've heard it said.'

'God doesn't only reside in churches, though,' he said. 'He's everywhere.'

'I sometimes wonder about that.'

'You have doubts?'

'Doesn't everyone from time to time?'

'Sometimes doubting is a sort of natural stop-off on the road to faith.'

'A bit like calling into the local saloon for a whiskey on your way to church, you mean?'

He gazed into her eyes. 'Are you ashamed of what you do?'

'Working in the saloon?'

He nodded.

'Why should I be?' She gave him a defiant look, then said, 'Yes, I suppose I am if I'm honest.'

'You just gave two answers to my question... Which one is the honest one?'

'Both of them.'

'That's impossible and contradictory.'

'Life's contradictory.'

'You're poking fun at me.'

'Not at all,' she said. 'Both answers can be true at different times... it sort of depends who's asking the question.'

'What about if *I* ask it?'

'I'd like to be something better than just a saloon girl.'

'You'd like to have a husband and a home of your own, start a family?'

'Show me the woman who wouldn't want all that?'

'Your tone suggests you think that would be asking too much.'

'Maybe it would.'

'Other women have those things.'

'Only I'm not other women – I'm Kate Bloom, saloon girl.'

'You don't have to be.'

'What choice do I have?'

'What if someone were to give you a choice?'

'Some cowboy's going to come and ask for my hand in marriage, you mean?' She smirked. 'Oh, I've had plenty of offers of that kind... ones that are made by some no-good sort between sundown and sunup...'

'I'm not talking about that sort of offer.'

'What are you talking about, then, Minister?'

His shyness had left him now, and he was confident with her; he felt as if they had known each other for a long time and that he was able to be natural with her and express his thoughts and feelings without fear of being misunderstood. It was as if the Minister in him had gone for a walk round the block, and now he was entirely Gene Sherrin. 'I'm talking about an offer from a man who is solvent and respectable and could offer you a home.'

'Would this be an offer of marriage?'

'It would indeed.'

She gazed at him with a mixture of awe and suspicion in her eyes. 'Are you saying I've got some secret admirer here in the parish,' she said, 'and this person's contacted you and asked you to approach me on his behalf?'

'Something like that.'

'And this secret admirer wants me to marry him?'

'He does indeed.

'In that case, I'd need to meet this secret admirer and see him with my own eyes,' she said, 'and hear him ask me to marry him.'

'Then what?'

'If I like the look of the man then, who knows? I might even give his offer some serious thought.'

'So you'd like to meet him?'

'Sure I would,' she said. 'But where is this man?'

'He's right here.'

'Where…?'

'You're looking at him.'

That's how the Minister came to woo Kate Bloom and ask for her hand in marriage, and she accepted him right there and then. They began to meet after that, to make plans for the future; and they decided to leave Kansas City and go some place new and marry there. That way, the Minister reasoned, they could turn over a new leaf and start out on their new life together.

He put in for a change of parish, and it turned out that the Minister in Monkford, had only recently passed away and they were waiting to be assigned a new preacher there. The parish was his if he wanted it. He accepted the offer, and the following day he and his new wife-to-be took their leave of Kansas City.

They married the following weekend, in Cold Springs, and Kate moved into the Minister's new house in Monkford; and so began their married life together. They were happy in a way that neither of them had really expected to be, and it wasn't long before Kate began to miss her monthlies and she realized she was pregnant.

They celebrated the news with a bottle of the finest champagne they could find in Monkford. Less than six weeks later, Kate was dead, and the baby she'd been expecting died along with her.

Chapter 9

Lucy Wilkes was loath to hang onto the desperado she was being forced to ride with, and that explained how she came to fall from the back of their mount. She fell awkwardly and hit the ground so hard that she lost consciousness for a time. When she came round, she was being hauled back onto the horse. Her ribs hurt terribly, and she wondered if she'd broken one or more of them. The pain was sufficient to cause her to fear another fall, and from then on she held onto the man's shirt or waist.

She wondered where they were taking her, and why they should want her with them; but whenever she asked them the first of these questions, they just said she'd find out. As to the second question, they reckoned the men in Fiveways would be wary of getting up a posse and coming after them, precisely because they had her with them. 'We catch so much of a sniff of those bastards,' Lee said, 'you're goan wish we hadn't, and them too.'

She didn't like the sound of this, but figured that she wasn't meant to. These were men who got what they wanted in life by making others fear them. The moment people stopped fearing them they would be nobodies, because they were the sort of useless scum who'd never be able to hold down a job of work or do anything halfway useful for anyone else. No, these men were all about serving themselves and their own needs and desires.

She wondered about this reason of theirs for bringing her along with them. They were using her to stop the men from trailing them. But surely her being with them would make the men want to come after them all the more, wouldn't it? She couldn't imagine John sitting on his hands and doing nothing. No, if she knew her husband, he would have gotten up a posse to come and find her. And the two sheriffs would come with him, wouldn't they? Sure they would. Otherwise, what was the point of their being sheriffs?

These thoughts gave her hope. If she could just sit tight and endure what was happening to her until John and the other men caught up with her, then she was sure they'd succeed in killing the three desperadoes, and she'd be able to go home with John and carry on with her life like none of this had happened. The desperadoes had talked of using her as a human shield, if anyone came after her; but she hoped it wouldn't come to that. John and the others would be alive to the risk of the desperadoes using her in that way, and so they'd know that they would have to surprise them.

As they rode over the dry rocky land, so the rhythm beat out by the hooves of the mount she shared with the gunslinger worked on her imagination rather like a drum, and she began to envisage seeing John again. She and John had been child-hood sweethearts, and he was the first and only man she'd ever loved. John had a regular job working at the bank, and he earned good enough money for them to buy a nice house with a garden in Fiveways. Lucy loved the rosebushes in her garden, and every time she thought of her home and of going back there she thought of those rosebushes.

She got thirsty after a while, but the men didn't give her any water and neither did she ask for any. She loathed the idea of asking them for anything: to do so would be to acknowledge her dependence on them, and this was a hateful notion to her. She was very conscious of her superiority to these men, in just about every conceivable way, with the exception of physical strength. That was the only thing they could better her at: they were stronger than her, and better with guns. But out here, in the Territory, where there was nobody around to come to her aid, physical strength and the ability to shoot were just about all that really counted.

She worried about her little daughter, Amy, and how John would cope with the job of bringing Amy up on his own if she didn't get out of this alive, and she tried to prevent herself from giving in to despair. It wasn't easy, but she had to stay positive, and trust to the fact that her husband John would come with a posse and free her from these hateful desperadoes. That was practically her only thought.

The men rode swiftly and without stopping to talk or discuss where they were headed, and this caused Lucy Wilkes to assume they must know where they were going. Nobody came out into the Territory but for Indians and the dregs of society, such as these three men, so it wasn't surprising perhaps that they should appear to know their way around. They finally stopped at sundown, and Lucy wondered about the sleeping arrangements. Needless to say, she was anxious that the men should leave her alone during the night, and tried not to allow thoughts of what they might conceivably be about to do to her to take shape in her imagination.

Her fear was such, though, that it was impossible for her to prevent such thoughts from entering her mind, and she began to pray to God, and to plead for His help. The men noticed that she was praying and seemed to be amused by it. The one dressed in black, Earl, sniggered and said, 'Why if the little lady here ain't askin' for some help from above.'

'Why so she is.' Lee leered at her and then his long lips curved in a wolfish grin. 'Ain't nobody up there goan help you none, sister.'

Lucy Wilkes continued to pray.

'Little lady thinks if she prays long and hard enough she goan summon a posse to come after us,' said Hank, the stocky one.

'That what it is, little missy?' Lee asked her. 'You prayin' your husband's goan come after us with a posse?'

She came to the end of her prayer and looked at the man. 'You've read my thoughts.'

Lee laughed. 'Well you're goan have to pardon me for my rudeness, ma'm, but that husband of yours didn't strike me as the kinda material be able to track us down.'

'Even if he was to,' Earl said, 'he'd be no match for us.'

'Perhaps he wouldn't on his own,' Lucy allowed. 'There are three of you, after all... but I doubt that he'd come alone.'

'Reckon there's men back in that rat hole of a town ready to stand up to the likes of us, do ya?'

'I can think of some that will.'

'Maybe so,' Earl said. 'But they goan have to find us first, little missy. And they don't know the Territory like we do.'

'One thing I do know, is that they'll stay on your trail until they find you.'

'Well I'll say if the little missy here don't know a lot of stuff.'

'I'll be darned if she don't,' Lee sniggered. 'Reckons she does, anyways.'

'Well it doesn't really matter what any of us says or thinks, does it?' Lucy said.

'And just what exac'ly's that suppose to mean, little missy?'

'What's going to happen's going to happen and that's it.'

'You're darn right there.' Lee looked over at Hank. 'Give her some water, then goan get what there is from the saddlebags and we'll cook somethin' up.'

Hank filled a tin mug with water and handed it to her, and she gulped it down.

The men cooked the sausages they'd brought with them over the fire, and then they began to eat them. 'Oh,' Lee said, 'I almost forgot, little missy. Here's yours.' He dropped the sausage onto a tin plate and offered it to her.

Lucy was aware of the way the men were all looking at her. 'Well,' Earl said, 'aren't you goan thank the man for givin' you his sausage?' He sniggered, and the other two men sniggered along with him.

She hated the men more than she'd ever hated anything or anyone. She wished them dead.

In any other circumstances, she would of course have refused the food, on account of the men's hateful ridicule; but now she was tempted to forget about the men and satisfy the hunger that was gnawing at her innards, for she hadn't eaten all day. Besides, she thought, food was clearly in short supply here. The men had brought some supplies with them, but they would soon run out and then there would be nothing. The desperadoes would be aware of this, she thought, and so maybe next time they ate they might not offer her anything. She swallowed her shame, and made to take the plate from the man's hand; but at that moment, he pulled it away.

'Ah-ah,' he said, 'I haven't heard you say thank you, yet.'

'Thank you.'

He sniggered and handed her the plate, and this time she took it and bit into the hot sausage meat. It tasted delicious, although she was sure that her hunger aided the taste somewhat. Soon it was all gone, and she was still hungry. The men ate three sausages each, but they didn't offer her any more.

They ate with the savage gusto of animals, so that Lucy wondered if these men had ever sat down at a table to eat a meal with decent people in all their lives. Why, their manners were no better than those of dogs, and they were much meaner than most of the dogs she'd ever come across.

When the men had finished eating, they looked at each other in a viciously conspiratorial way that struck fear into Lucy's heart. Neither of them said anything, but it was as though their faces spoke volumes. She hoped and prayed that she was only imagining things, and that the men were not really as bad as she feared them to be. She hoped that John and the posse he must surely have got up were on their trail, and that they would arrive any moment and put a stop to whatever it was the three desperadoes had in mind. Because she sensed, with a woman's intuition, that they were bent on evil.

The men kept shooting fierce glances at each other; it was like they were acting out some kind of bestial ritual, rather the way certain animals make a show of strength before they fight, or sometimes instead of fighting. Then the lanky one, Lee, got up on his knees and moved over to where she was sitting. 'What do you want?' she asked, without daring to look at him.

'Well I wonder now?' he said. 'What d'you reckon I might be wantin', little missy?'

'Please, don't,' she said. 'I'm not that sort of woman.'

'We'll see about that.' With that, he launched himself on her. She lashed out with her hands and tried to kick him, in an effort to fight him off; but then Hank pinned her wrists to the ground, and Earl took her by the ankles. Lee pulled her dress up and she felt him tearing at her underwear. 'Please, don't! No!' she cried. 'I'm a married woman and a mother.'

The men paid her no heed. 'Why you ungrateful wench,' Lee said. 'Just fed you to keep you alive, didn't I? Now you goan give me somethin' in return.'

Her skirt was up over her head now, and she screamed as one of them pushed her ankles up so that her knees were bent and apart; and she felt the awful, beastly man begin to do things to her - things that she'd only ever allowed John to do – and then he entered her. He was rough and hurt her, so that her cries were full of pain, as well as terror and anger. She hated this man more than she thought it possible for her ever to hate anyone or anything, and just wanted it to stop; but he kept lunging at her and hurting her, and then suddenly it was over. But the next moment, it was starting again, and she realized that they were all going to have their fun with her.

These men were worse than beasts, she thought. Why, John was a man, but what he did with her when they were in bed at night had nothing to do with what these men were doing to her now. John was gentle and tender, and he made love to her in a way that always left her feeling how much he cared for her. He made her feel special somehow. But these men were taking all that special feeling and tearing it up and throwing it in the dust. They were taking everything that was good and decent in the world and making a mockery of it. They were taking the very act of love itself, and making a hateful thing of it. Because their lovemaking had no love in it at all; it was made of nothing but hatred and derision. And all it would ever inspire in Lucy's heart was more hatred.

That was the terrible thing: they weren't just doing a hateful thing here, but they were also desecrating the most wonderful thing in life, and so this thing that was happening to her was doubly bad. Somehow the three men seemed to sense this, the way animals sense things; but their intuition of the great evil they were doing served only to drive them on to do more evil. It was as if evil served only to beget more evil, and hatred to beget more hatred. Lucy felt herself descending into a pit where there was nothing but evil and vileness and viciousness. It was not an actual pit but it was no less real for that. You might say it was an emotional pit, one of the heart. It was as if she could feel darkness descending upon her soul. Where was the good Lord that the Minister in Fiveways talked of now? she wondered. Where was her guardian angel in her time of need? And what about John? Why wasn't he here when she needed him?

When the second man finished, the third one started in. She cried as he speared her tender rawness, but he only hissed evil things back at her. He seemed to think she was enjoying it and took her cries as an incitement to lunge at her with ever greater violence. She told herself that this man was the third one, so when he'd finished what he was doing they would leave her alone and bed down for the night. At least then she would be able to sleep and in so doing find a little respite from the horror of her predicament. But no sooner had the third one finished than the first one began again. She could tell it was him by the sound of his voice as he hissed filthy phrases full of evil into her ear. He was the lanky one, by the name of Lee. They were all evil, the three of them; but she fancied if one of them was worse than the others it was this man. He seemed to be the leader of the three, so far as she could make out. Not that they appeared to have assigned that role to him in any definite or formal way; it was just that he had a way of talking that made the others listen. Maybe they feared what would happen to them if they didn't. And he'd been the first one to force himself on her and start off this riot of evil.

She told herself she would get even with the man if it was the last thing she did. She cursed him as he hacked away at her. For this man, it was clear that love and violence were all part and parcel of the same thing. He didn't know what love was, only violence. And the violence that filled his heart was what he had instead of love. Just as you couldn't expect to find water and pretty plants and flowers in a wilderness, so you couldn't expect to find gentleness or compassion in the heart of a man like this one. He was in his element, out here in the Territory, where all was dryness and rock and lizards and rattlers and cactus plants. It was as if he had the desert in his heart. Maybe this land was the devil, she thought. Maybe the desert was the root of all evil. Maybe it was the desert that good men and women had to fight against, and stop encroaching on their lives. The desert had eaten up this man and his two companions. They weren't fit to live anyplace else, just as you wouldn't want to have rattlers living in a town. They had all the compassion and decency in their hearts that you might expect to find in your average rattler. They were scum.

He finished with a great hacking fury of violence, then rolled off her over onto his back, and the next one took over. They carried on like that for what seemed like an eternity. Then when they'd finally had their fill, they left her alone.

Lee leered at her and tipped his hat, which he'd kept on all the while, in an evil mockery of decency and respect. 'Thankin' you kindly, missy, for serving me and my two friends. We appreciate it.' He looked at the other two. 'Don't we, boys?'

'Sure we do, little missy,' said Earl.

Hank chuckled. 'Man has his needs, and God put nice little women like you on this earth to service 'em.'

There were a lot of things she might have said to these three, but Lucy realized that she would have been wasting her breath. Besides, she was exhausted. In fact, she couldn't remember ever having been so tired in all her life. She supposed this was why they'd brought her with them, or at least one of the reasons. She was here for their entertainment, and she supposed they would keep her alive so long as they wanted to use her. She had never been made to feel like this before. The men had taken her heart and soul and trampled it in the dust. They had made her feel like she was just a thing, an object to be possessed and used. What she might think or feel about the ways in which she was being used, was of no interest to them. She had no right to complain; at any rate, if she did so then her words would fall on deaf ears. Now she was one with the Territory. The wilderness had emptied her heart of all that had been good in there and filled it with emptiness. The good things of this world, she realized, did not come into being or happen of themselves; they were the work of decent men and women, who strove to work together for the general good. The goodness that she had known in Monkford had not, as she'd previously believed, been the goodness that was natural to mankind; no, everything that made life worth living was brought into being by dint of a thousand and one little sacrifices and acts of kindness, the sacrifices and acts of kindness of people who were good and decent; people who were constantly on guard against the desert and who were prepared to wage their own personal wars against it, to stop it making inroads into their own hearts. The true meaning of civilization was nothing more than human kindness and generosity, and the creation of civilization involved a tremendous effort; because the desert was the natural state of things, she now realized. The desert had no heart or feelings. The desert was Godless. It was a hostile force, inimical to civilizing forces of any color or persuasion. That was why it took such strength and courage for a person to grow strong and decent. Because men and women were not naturally good or strong or decent. They were naturally like the pieces of scum who'd brought her out here into the wilderness, to use her according to their own whims. Now all she had to do was forget the good and decent part of herself and be like the three desperadoes and things would be a lot easier for her. It was simple, really, she decided. All I need to do is allow myself to sink to the lowest level, and allow myself to blend with the wilderness and become one with it. I need to become a piece of scum like these three men and then I won't suffer so much. And yet, if she surrendered the best part of herself then she realized everything that had ever made her life worth living would be gone.

But it's already gone, you fool, she told herself. Do you really think there's any way back for you? This is the end of the road.

The men tied her hands and feet before bedding down for the night. She asked them why there was any need for this. 'Where do you think I'm going to run away to?'

'Ain't nothin' but emptiness any direction you go, missy,' Lee said.

'So why do you need to tie me up?'

He leered at her. 'No sayin' what ideas you might get in your head while we sleepin'.'

So he knows my thoughts, she thought. He knows that I will kill him the first chance I get.

She fell asleep straightaway but slept fitfully. She dreamed about what happened to her and woke up screaming, only to find herself lying out under the stars. Had it all just been a nightmare? she wondered. But then she saw the three men lying there. Two of them, Earl and Hank, had slept through her screams, but Lee was awake and he looked over at her. 'What's the matter, little missy, did somethin' nasty bite ya?' He laughed, as if he reckoned he was funny.

She turned over and willed herself to go back to sleep, but the nightmare that had woken her was so dreadful a part of her was loath to sleep again. Not that being awake gave her any more cause to find hope for a better tomorrow.

Chapter 10

Sheriff Hawkins was wondering about the Wilkes woman as he lay there, under the stars. He just hoped those three desperadoes were at least showing the poor woman a modicum of respect in their treatment of her; although somehow he feared that this might not be the case. He glanced over at the woman's husband, John Wilkes, and saw that he was awake, too.

'Can't sleep, either, Sheriff?' Wilkes said.

'Just woke up,' Hawkins lied. 'You'd better get some shut-eye or you'll be too exhausted to get on the trail tomorrow.'

'I could say the same to you.'

Hawkins shut his eyes and willed himself to fall asleep, but the same thoughts get going around and around in his mind. He remembered the way the three desperadoes had beaten and kicked the Minister, in the main drag in Monkford, and how the man's wife had come to his aid; and then how she'd picked up the gun of the man who'd fallen, and fired it, then her body had gone kind of stiff like she was frozen in ice or something and she fell. She was a good, brave woman. He'd heard a rumor that she'd worked as a saloon girl in Kansas City before she married the Minister, and that the couple had moved to Monkford to start again fresh, and give her the opportunity to play the role of respectable housewife without having people cast aspersions on her good name. Well, Sheriff Hawkins didn't give a darn about whether the woman had been a saloon girl or not; he reckoned there were moments in a person's life when they revealed their true selves, and in those moments during the shootout in the street, back in Monkford, the woman had shown what she was made of all right, and all of it was mighty fine material. Why, she'd shown more selfless courage than most of the men in the town put together. Old Hollis, the storekeeper, had borne up well; despite always having appeared to be the quiet, timid sort, he'd got his gun out and shown he had some balls. He'd lost his life in the gunfight, but he'd died a man's death and his people could be proud of him.

He hadn't been like those bastards who'd come down from the rooms in the saloon, when he'd gone in there after it was all over. The yella sonsofbitches came down acting like they didn't know what had happened; but Hawkins reckoned different. They knew all right: they'd just preferred to stay up in those rooms than get their asses out of bed and grab a gun. But the Sherrin woman had the balls to grab one all right.

Sheriff Hawkins felt sorry for the woman's husband, too. The Minister was a good man, and he'd tried to stand up to the desperadoes in his own way. Trouble was, the man's way wasn't the one that was ever going to work with pieces of human scum like that. The Minister had tried to appeal to the men's better nature – something those desperadoes just didn't have. Minister's problem was, he just believed in human nature too much; he seemed to think there was good in everyone, and all you had to do was seek it out. Well, you could do a lot of searching where some folk were concerned and never come close to finding anything decent. The Sheriff knew this for a fact, because he'd had to deal with some real nasty specimens in his time. Types who only listened to reason and did the right thing when you pointed a gun at them.

What made things worse, he knew for a fact that the Minister's love for his wife, Kate, had been deep and sincere. And now the poor man would have to face his congregation next Sunday and preach the word of God, and the need to turn the other cheek and all that bunkum, and all the while he'd have the thought of what happened to his Kate gnawing away at his innards; and it would be like that for him for the rest of his days. How would the man ever manage to keep his faith? Hawkins wondered. Perhaps he wouldn't. Perhaps he'd grow angry with the good Lord and shake his fist at Him, and demand an explanation for what happened, or an apology. Some kind of sign - *something*, anyway. Hawkins knew that he sure as hell would.

The Minister was a good sort, Hawkins reckoned, and in some ways the man reminded him of himself. Whereas I'm trying to represent the rule of law in Monkford, he thought, the Minister's busy laying down God's law. They were two different kinds of law, for sure: the one sought to implement earthly justice and the other worked more in the realm of eternity. The Sheriff had never quite been able to get a handle on the notion of eternity. Whenever he tried to think about it, his head would spin, almost like it did sometimes when he'd taken a drop too much whiskey. So we're different, the two of us, he thought, and yet we've got things in common. Both of us are trying to make things better, because a world without laws would be just like living in the Territory. The strong would have free rein while they preyed on the weak, and there would be no justice or sense in anything. Sheriff Hawkins hated the very *thought* of living in such a world. He imagined the three gunslingers he was trailing would like it fine. They represented everything that was evil and wrong in the world, in his eyes, and he promised himself once more that he would bring them to justice or die trying. He wasn't doing this for the good men of Monkford, few of whom were really very good at all, or deserving of a decent sheriff even; no, he was doing it for himself, and for Kate Sherrin and the Minister, and Hollis, the storekeeper, and all the other good and decent people in the world. He had no idea whether there really was a God, and if there was then whether He was keeping a watchful eye over him. Perhaps there was no God at all, and that was all a load of wishful thinking; the Sheriff wouldn't have been surprised. But whatever the truth was on that score, he was sure that he believed in decent folk and in knowing the difference between right and wrong, and not just knowing that much but standing up for what was right.

Harvey Boyle had been a good man, and he was darn good sheriff, too; but they hadn't even been able to give him a proper burial. We did the best we could in the circumstances, though, Hawkins thought, and with that he fell asleep.

Meanwhile, John Wilkes was still awake. He'd been lying there with his eyes closed, trying to will himself to drop off; but sometimes, the harder you tried the more difficult it was. You had to let sleep come to you; try to will it along its way and it would likely turn on its heel and go off in the other direction, leave you lying there and wondering when it was going to come back. Women could be like that, too, John Wilkes sometimes had occasion to think. Lucy could, anyway. But he loved his wife to distraction, and the thought that those three men had her with them right now gave him no rest. He prayed to God that they wouldn't touch her. Maybe they weren't as bad as they seemed, he thought. Oh, they were bad all right, that much was clear. But maybe they'd at least know to respect a woman who was a wife and a mother. And then as a religious man, he knew that God must be watching down on him and Lucy and the three men who had her, and that He would surely play a hand in all this. But how would He set about doing that? John Wilkes wondered. Would the Almighty see to it that he and his two companions would finally catch up on the desperadoes and overpower them, so he could take Lucy back home with him? Sure He would, because if He didn't then where was the sense in believing in Him? And if there was no point in believing in Him, then why had so many people all over the world have done so down through the generations? All those people couldn't be wrong, could they? No, of course they couldn't. And so that meant God would find a way to make everything come out right. There was a kind of natural logic to it, John Wilkes saw. And that natural logic tended always to work for the general good.

He'd known Lucy since they were both little kids. Back in those days, they used to play together, along with the other children in the neighboring houses. John's favorite game had always been Cowboys and Indians and he'd always wanted to take the part of the cowboy, so that it had often fallen to poor Lucy to be the Indian. He recalled how she used to complain and say she was sick of always being a baddie. 'But you're my squaw,' John used to tell her, to try and smooth things over. 'Cowboys can sometimes take a squaw for a wife and then she's no longer a baddie.'

'But I don't want to be nobody's squaw,' Lucy would say. 'I want to be a sheriff like you, and get to wear a tin badge and carry a Winchester.'

Whenever she said that, it would always fall to John to try and make her see reason. 'But you can't, Lucy,' he'd say. 'Everyone knows you have to be a boy to be Sheriff.'

'But I've got blonde hair,' he recalled Lucy telling him one time. 'How can you have a squaw that's got blonde hair?'

'We'll just have to pretend you've got black hair,' he told her.

Poor Lucy, it was a sad state of affairs really, and quite unfair – even he'd come to see that much eventually. But there it was. Then over time they'd drifted apart somehow, and the old games of Cowboys and Indians were a thing of the past. They'd see each other in church on a Sunday and maybe say hello, ask how things were going. Around that time he started to feel differently about Lucy, started to see things in her that he just hadn't noticed before. While in the old days, he'd always felt a little sorry for her, what with her always wanting to be Sheriff and never getting to be one, somehow she'd grown quite different in the intervening years. There was a kind of beauty and glamour about her that he'd never had cause to notice before; maybe it had never even been there before, for all he knew, because at that time, being only fourteen, he really didn't know very much about girls and their ways at all. He wondered where it had all come from, this new stuff she had. Wherever she'd got it, he realized that she now possessed a certain power to charm and even dazzle him, so that on occasion he would find himself looking at her and wondering if he'd been misled and seen what wasn't really there. Maybe it was all just a trick of the light or something, he thought, because Lucy couldn't really be *that* pretty, now could she? In order to try to keep a grip, he reminded himself that she was just plain old Lucy Morgan, and that there was really nothing very special or extraordinary about her. She was just the girl who'd wanted to be Sheriff, that's all. But somehow thinking this way didn't help him much now, because he still got to feeling dazzled by her whenever he looked at her; and no, it wasn't a trick of the light or anything of that sort. He knew, because he'd looked at her long and hard a few times, and she *kept on* being beautiful all the while. In short, he was enamored of her, and began to feel rather foolish in her presence. Now when she spoke to him he would often get a little embarrassed or even tongue-tied and, what made things worse, he would sometimes catch her grinning at him, like she found his predicament rather amusing. When this happened, the sense of shame and humiliation that took hold of him knew no bounds, and he would get so mad with himself and with her that he'd almost start to look on her as if she were his enemy. But that was ridiculous, of course, and just him being a stupid little kid; because Lucy was a lovely girl with a nice nature, and it wasn't her fault if she'd grown pretty, was it?

He remembered that first time he'd kissed her. They'd been out walking on a lovely evening in April, and spring had been in the air; and somehow they'd been talking and he'd got the feeling that he might kiss her if he wanted to. He had no idea what had given him this idea – when in fact, Lucy had been trying to suggest it to him by staring at his lips - and he'd been sorely tempted to chance his arm; but he was always timid by nature, and it proved no different on this occasion. Thoughts of what she might think or do if he made his move and she didn't like it held him back – or they would have done, had Lucy not decided to take the reins and start the kissing. He'd just turned fifteen, and it was the first time he'd ever kissed any girl, and it was so nice that he hadn't wanted it to stop. Things progressed quickly between the pair of them after that, and they got married as soon as they were old enough; by then he already had his job in the bank, and life was good. He remembered their warm nights in bed, the tenderness that he'd always felt for his wife; and perhaps his imagination was ever working overtime a little, because he seemed to remember everything like it had been even better than it was.

And now those three desperadoes had taken her. Well, John Wilkes was no man of violence. Truth to tell, he'd never fired a shot in anger in his entire life. But he would only be too pleased to fire those three bastards all the way down to Hell, just as soon as he got close enough to be able to draw a bead on them. He finally fell asleep with this thought in mind and dreamed about Lucy. They were at home of an evening to begin with, and he was reading the newspaper while Lucy was sitting with their daughter Amy on her lap and teaching her to read; and then everything changed in his dream and the three desperadoes were holding him and the other men at gunpoint in the house back in Fiveways, while they got the Doc to take the bullet out of the arm of the one of their number that was wounded. John Wilkes made a move on the lanky one in his dream, and managed to knock the pistol out of his hand; then he began to wrestle the man for the gun. While this was going on, the stocky one called

Hank held his gun to John Wilkes's head, and Wilkes realized that the game was up.

He opened his eyes, and wondered for a moment whether he was still dreaming. 'Get up nice and slow, cowboy,' a voice said, and John Wilkes realized that he wasn't dreaming.

'Any fast moves and you're dead... now on your feet.'

'Okay, mister. Just don't shoot.' He got up, taking care not to make any jerky movements, just like the man said. 'Who are you?'

'That's my business.'

'What do your want?'

'That's a better question,' the man said. 'First, undo your belt and drop it to the ground – and remember, I've got my gun against the back of your head. One false move and you're gone.'

'All right.' John Wilkes undid his belt and allowed it to fall to the floor. 'Now kick it away from you.' John Wilkes obliged, and the man moved round him, then bent his knees and slowly hunkered down, keeping his back straight and his gun pointed at John Wilkes. He took Wilkes's gun out of the holster, and straightened up to his full height once more. 'You're mighty sensible,' the man said. 'Where you men from?'

'Fiveways.'

'Nice little town.'

'Was the last time we robbed the bank there, Jeff,' said the man's accomplice, who had been busy relieving Deputy Joe of his guns.

'You won't get away with this,' Joe said.

'Well I'll be blowed if yer man's not had the audacity to express an opinion, Matt.'

'And to our contrary, Jeff, if I understood him right.'

Joe said, 'You understood me right, mister.'

'Got balls as well as a tin badge.'

'Shame he ain't got no brains to go with 'em.'

'He had brains, he wouldn't be where he is.'

'It's not you we're after,' Joe said. 'If you leave now then we'll let you get on your way.'

'Well that's might kindly of you, mister,' said Jeff. 'Don't you reckon that's mighty kindly of the man, Matt?'

'Yes, Jeff, I'd have to say it's mighty kindly of the man.'

'Not very bright but kindly.'

'Exac'ly.'

Joe said, 'It's different men we're after.'

'Which different men would these be?'

'The ones who robbed the people in the church at Monkford on Sunday morning, then left Fiveways with the good lady wife of my companion here.'

'Is that so?'

'We aim to liberate the lady and bring the men to justice.'

'Do you now?'

'We sure do.'

'Sounds very noble of you, mister.'

'So you see, we ain't got no beef with you two... and nor have we got the time or the inclination to be followin' your trail, so long as you leave now.'

'All sounds very interestin', mister.'

'Just tellin' it like it is,' Joe said. 'You men might be a bad lot, but we're after three types who're a lot worse.'

Jeff chuckled. 'You hear that, Matt?'

'I heard it, Jeff.'

'This man's picked up the idea we ain't all bad.'

'That's nice.'

'I think so, too.' Jeff seemed to find all this terribly amusing. 'Have to get this man to write me a character reference.'

'Show it to all the sheriffs in the towns roundabouts.'

'Before we rob the banks in 'em, you mean?'

'Least that way,' said Matt, 'they'd know it was good people robbed them banks.'

'Got a point there, Matt.'

'Better get the guns off the man over there's sleepin', before he wakes up, Jeff.'

'Wouldn't want a nasty surprise, now would you?' said Sheriff Hawkins. 'Now put your guns down, the pair of you.'

'That's a mighty funny joke you just told, mister.'

'It wasn't a joke and it wasn't funny. I've got my gun pointed at you both,' Sheriff Hawkins said to Jeff. 'Either you do as I say or I'll shoot the pair of you.'

'Now why'd you wanna goan do a dumb thing like that?'

'I can think of lots of reasons.'

'I can think of two why you shouldn't,' Jeff said, 'and they standin' right here in front of us. You fire that thing and these two are dead.'

'Along with you two.'

Matt said, 'I'd take you out, mister, before you know it.'

'I didn't get to be a sheriff and stay one for this long without having to shoot a lot of people who wanted to shoot me.'

'That tin badge don't impress me none.'

'I wouldn't expect it to,' Hawkins said. 'But my six-shooters'll make short work of the pair of you if you don't drop your guns.'

'But there's no need for any of this,' Jeff said. 'If you shoot us and we shoot you then we all lose out… You was a sensible man, you'd let us take want we want and go.'

'And what would that be?'

'Little food and water… and any money you've got, and your guns and ammo.'

'We'd be as good as dead out here if we agreed to that, you rat.'

'We'd leave you enough food and water to last till you get to the next town.'

'The next town's a long way from here, mister.'

'We'd leave you your horses.'

The Sheriff didn't believe them. He fired both his guns at the men. He got the one called Jeff in the chest, and the man fell to the ground, dead. But he only got the other man, Matt, in his arm, on account of not being such a good shot with his left hand. The man fired when the Sheriff did and his shot got Hawkins in the gut. The Sheriff felt the blow like a kick from a horse. He fired again, and the man dropped onto his knees. The man aimed his gun at Hawkins and was about to fire, but John Wilkes moved fast and kicked the gun out of his hand; then he kicked the man again. The man groaned and just lay there, looking like he was either unconscious or dead. John Wilkes grabbed the man's gun and shot him in the head. The man was dead now all right. John Wilkes now turned his attention to the second man; but it was all right: he was already dead, too.

That was the good news.

The bad news was, Deputy Joe Davison looked like he'd been hit. He hunkered down by Joe and began to shake him. 'Come on, Joe,' he said, 'don't you give out on me now, you hear?'

But Joe wasn't going to hear anything ever again. He was dead.

John Wilkes turned his attention to Sheriff Hawkins. 'You hit, Sheriff?' he asked.

'Took one in the gut,' the Sheriff groaned.

John Wilkes knew that it sounded bad. His mind was reeling. He'd never been in a situation like this before, where he'd had to tend to a man who had been shot, and he didn't have much idea about what to do. He grabbed the water canteen. 'Here,' he said, 'try and drink a little.'

'No, they say not to drink anything with a gut wound.'

'I'll need to get you to the nearest town.'

'I'll never make it, John. You go without me.'

'I can't do that, Sheriff.'

'You've got to.'

'But I'm not just going to leave you here like this.'

'You can leave me with my gun.'

'I'm not going to do that, Sheriff.'

'It's the only hope you've got, John... You should turn back and go get more help.'

'Don't talk like that, Sheriff.'

'It's no good, John. I haven't got much time.'

'You're going to be all right.'

'Listen to me, John.' Sheriff Hawkins grabbed at John Wilkes's shirt. 'You need to turn back, do you hear me?'

'But I can't... What about Lucy?'

'I want you to promise me.'

'I need to find Lucy.'

'You can't go after those desperadoes on your own, John,' Hawkins said. 'You'd never find them, for a start... And even if you did, they outnumber you three to one. You wouldn't stand a chance.'

'But I've got to try.'

'Listen to me, John,' Sheriff Hawkins was talking slowly now and having to make a great effort. 'You need to go back to Five-ways and get another posse up... Tell everyone there about what's happened.'

'But nobody would come here with me, if I told them that.'

'You can't do it on your own, John.' Sheriff Hawkins pulled hard on John Wilkes's shirt. 'Promise me,' he said. Then his fingers loosened their grip, and he fell back and his head struck the ground.

'Sheriff, you just hang on in there, you hear?'

The Sheriff didn't say anything.

John Wilkes began to shake him.

Still the Sheriff didn't say anything.

The Sheriff was dead.

Chapter 11

John Wilkes buried the bodies of his two travelling companions and said a prayer for them. He prayed to God to give him strength and the good fortune to find the three desperadoes, so that he could spring Lucy from their clutches and take her home with him. This was the only thought in his mind now.

He boiled up some water in a pan over the open fire, and made himself coffee, which he drank from a tin cup. He helped himself to some bread from the provisions they'd brought with them, and broke the bread up into bits and dropped it into the coffee; then he ate it with a spoon.

The sun came up while he was having his breakfast. He gathered together all of the provisions they'd brought with them and put them in his saddlebag, then mounted his horse and set off. He reckoned the desperadoes must have headed on west with Lucy, and so the thing to do was keep on going that way. Sooner or later, he would be sure to run across them. He based this conclusion on some rather simple logic: to the south the land was full of Indians, and to the north the mountains rose across the skyline in the distance.

He rode all day and by lunchtime the sun was fierce as a bastard, and there was no hiding from it out here. The land was dry, with patches of scrub and cactuses here and there, and the heat shimmered on the horizon. The sweat was pouring off him by now, and he would have done anything to come across a river that he'd be able to stop and swim in. He had a fair bit of water left, but he had to be sure to ration it, because there was no telling how long he was going to be out here like this; and once his water was all gone, then there was nowhere you could go to get any more. He stopped at one point to let his horse drink. He poured some water into a saucepan and held it up to the animal's mouth as it drank. Then he patted the horse on the head. He felt sorry for it, having to be out here in this heat and carrying him around; and besides, he knew that if his horse gave out then it would be all up for him, too. If being out in land like this on your own taught you anything, it was the importance of getting along with your horse, and of the importance of the animal to you.

All this was new to John Wilkes, who until now had lived what many might call a sheltered life. He'd never had cause to leave Fiveways, except to visit Cold Springs and Monkford and a few of the other towns in the vicinity, and his had been a happy, settled and ordered existence. Working as he had in the bank from a young age, he had been used to his desk with his in and out tray. He'd never had cause to fire a shot in anger, either, until he'd come out here. But he'd killed a man during the night. He wondered how he felt about it, and figured he didn't really feel all that much. He'd heard folk say that a man could get to feeling down in the dumps after he'd taken a life for the first time; but if John Wilkes was feeling upset about anything, then it was the thought that the three desperadoes had his wife, and that those other two bastards that had come to try and rob them in the night had killed his two travelling companions. He felt bad about losing Bill Hawkins and Sheriff Joe, all right, and Sheriff Boyle before that; but not about killing the desperado. The man would have killed me if I hadn't killed him, he thought. I had no choice. If anything, he was rather pleased with the way he'd acted; the fact that he'd done what needed to be done, without pausing or faltering.

He rode on through the dry land with the stubborn determination of a man driven by a single idea. He was going to find the desperadoes and kill them, and then take Lucy home with him. All right, there were three of them and only one of him, but he had the element of surprise on his side, and he reckoned that evened things up a little. He'd need some luck, if things were to go his way; he knew that. But the way he saw it, there was no alternative. The Sheriff had tried to get him to promise to return to Fiveways and get up another posse, but he doubted any of the men there would want to come out here with him – especially once they'd heard what had happened to the three men he came out here with. Four men go out there and only one comes back, and now he wants us to go back there with him, they'd say. They'd consider the odds and then they'd shake their heads and say sorry, they'd like to go but they had a family. Or else this or else that: they'd all have some excuse or other. He knew what the men in Fiveways were like, having lived there all his life; and knowing them as he did, he knew there was hardly a man among them that wasn't yellow, with the exception of Sheriff Harvey and his Deputy. And now those two men had gone to meet their Maker. It's all up to me, he told himself. There's no turning back. I'm Lucy's last hope.

John Wilkes rode for three days without seeing a soul. He came across a corpse that had been flayed – by Indians, he supposed – and was now being eaten by vultures. The sight would have deterred a man driven by a less stubborn sense of purpose, but John Wilkes was not for turning back. Not until he'd found his Lucy. He was a good man driven by a single idea and impulse: to save his wife from the bastards that had taken her.

He was riding through a narrow gulch when someone opened fire on him from the rocks. The bullet missed him but got his horse, and it went down, so that he had to jump to prevent himself from falling under it, and he hit the rocky ground with a thump. The fall would have hurt him had he not known that he'd better move fast or he'd be a dead man. He clambered to his feet and reached for his gun, when a lasso came flying out of the rocks from behind him and looped over his head. Next thing he knew, the rope tightened over his arms so that he was unable to move them; then he found himself being pulled. He tried to stand his ground, and managed to do so for a short while; then three men climbed down from the crevices they'd concealed themselves in.

The tall one, Lee, said, 'Glad to see you finally caught up with us, John.'

'It's you three,' John Wilkes said, and his heart sank.

'Frankly, I didn't think you had it in you to ever find us... I'm impressed.'

'Where's Lucy?'

'She's all right,' Earl said. 'We been takin' real good care of her for you.' He looked at Lee. 'Ain't that right, partner?'

'Sure is.' Lee grinned. 'No need to worry on that score, John. We been givin' that little lady of yours all the attention she needs.'

'Let us go,' John Wilkes said. 'We haven't done anything to you, and you've nothing to gain by holding us or killing us.'

Lee walked up to John Wilkes and hit him hard on the side of the head with the handle of his pistol, and John Wilkes went down. When he came round, sometime later, he was strapped to a horse. They were no longer in the gulch but out in the open plain, and they were no longer moving. He could hear a woman's screams. It's Lucy, he thought, and craning his neck he saw her. She was lying on the dry, rocky ground, and the tall man, Lee, was forcing himself on her. 'You can't do that,' John Wilkes screamed. 'You can't rape my wife like that!'

The men laughed. After Lee had finished, the stocky one, Hank, took over; and then, when he'd had enough, the one in black, Earl, took his turn. All the while John Wilkes was screaming like a madman. He called on the good Lord for divine help, but none was forthcoming and the desperadoes just kept on with what they were doing to Lucy. John Wilkes supposed the three of them had been raping his wife when they fancied ever since the time they took her. It was all too much for him. He cursed the three men and God and the world and everyone in it. He wished he'd never been born.

When they'd finished with Lucy, they got John Wilkes down off the horse and forced him down onto the ground; then Earl and Hank held him, and Lee did to him what he'd done to Lucy. John Wilkes screamed and cursed God, and his wife Lucy screamed and cursed along with him while all this was going on.

After Lee had finished, he invited the other two men to take their turn. 'I guess I'm just more particular when it comes to that kinda thing than you are, Lee,' Hank said. 'But the truth is, I never much liked the idea of stickin' my equipment inside the ass of another man.'

'Me neither,' Earl sniggered. 'But each to his own.'

Lee shrugged and zipped himself up. 'Don't know about you,' he said, 'but I've had enough of these two and their whinin'.' He took out his gun and shot Lucy in the head. John Wilkes began to scream, and Lee shot him in the gut.

John Wilkes suffered in agony for the next four hours or so, before he finally breathed his last and went to meet his Maker. By that time, the three desperadoes were making their way back east, Lee having decided there couldn't be any posse coming after them, seeing as John Wilkes had shown up on their trail alone like he did.

'Dunno about you boys,' he said, 'but I fancy the idea of spendin' me some time in Dodge, and payin' a visit on some of the saloon girls they got there.'

Earl and Hank reckoned that sounded like a mighty fine idea.

On their way back through the Territory, they came across the bodies of four men who'd been scalped. The faces of these four had been eaten away by vultures and vermin, but they'd once belonged to Byron Towers, Steve Williams, Dan Riley and Chris Collins.

Looking at the half-eaten bodies, Earl said, 'Work of Indians.'

'Better keep an eye out,' Lee said.

Chapter 12

Back in Monkford life went on much as usual, and the townsfolk tried to put the events of that terrible day behind them. Many of them seemed to act as if they only had to pretend none of it had ever happened and it would be as if it really had never happened. Some might say this was not only a sensible attitude to adopt but the right one in the circumstances. These were men of peace, who wanted nothing more than to be able to live out their lives doing the simple things they had always done. They were proud of their town and of the part they played in its daily life. Or at least they had been, until that fateful day. But what was pride? You couldn't touch it or eat it, and neither could you sell it. Pride was something and nothing, these men decided. It was a notion that young men who knew little of the world and its ways were apt to get into their heads; then when they got a little experience under their belts and learned better, they usually changed their tune. Pride was also a ridiculous thing to have, looked at in that way; it had no real place in an ordered society, where decent men and women went about their various tasks and strove for the general good. Pride was all about the individual. It was for hotheaded men with big egos. Men who were too big for their britches, as the saying went. Why, didn't it even say as much, if in different words, in the Holy Bible? Was a Christian not called upon, as the Minister had said in his sermons, to turn the other cheek? In this way, the good people of Monkford tended to their wounded pride. Nobody spoke of what had happened, because to do so would have been to go against the grain, to break a sort of silent agreement that the people of the town had taken to put the past behind them and move on. And so the townsfolk lived like people who are sworn to secrecy, and they assumed the mask of Christian morality in doing so. Their behavior and general attitude seemed to say they felt they were superior to men of violence and their low ways, and indeed, this was no doubt true; but even so, something ate away at the townsfolk, so that everyone felt there was something very wrong with the town of Monkford and its citizens. Everything might seem all right on the surface, but there was trouble brewing down in the deep water.

Of course everyone in Monkford knew about what had happened in Fiveways: how the three gunslingers had gone there to get the one of their number who was wounded treated by Doc Monk, but he was drunk and so they'd had to come and get Doc Waters. The people all knew this, and they knew also that Sheriff Hawkins had gone there along with the Doc. They knew, too, about what happened next, and how Sheriff Hawkins and three men from Fiveways had gone on the trail of the three desperadoes who'd taken a woman from Fiveways with them; but they had heard no news of what had happened to Sheriff Hawkins and his companions. Neither had they heard anything about the four men from Monkford that had gone after the desperadoes, and if the truth were known they didn't *want* to hear anything. They feared that the men would all come to a bad end, as so often happened to those who went off into the Territory, and this was another thing that weighed on the collective conscience of the townsfolk.

In their time of need, the townsfolk looked more than ever to the church for moral as well as spiritual support and guidance. The townsfolk needed to hear the Minister tell them that they had done, and were continuing to do, the right thing. They needed to hear it from him, and they needed to hear him tell them that this was the word of the good Lord. They loved it when the Minister preached of the need to turn the other cheek, because then they could go home sure in the knowledge that they had nothing to feel guilty about.

But something strange happened: just when the townsfolk needed the Minister to be strong for them, he appeared to be about to falter. And what was even odder: he seemed to falter in a spiritual sense, even while he regained his physical health. Come the beginning of December, the Minister's broken bones had healed and he was able to walk and move as well as he'd ever done; but when you heard him talk, you knew there was something different about him. It was as if there were a big wound festering deep inside him. If you paid heed to the man, you got the feeling he was trying to tend to the wound, but somehow it just kept getting bigger. This wound wasn't a physical but rather a spiritual and emotional one, and it was proving resistant to the Minister's own efforts to cure it by taking heed of the lessons that were to be learned from the Holy Bible. It was there in the way the man moved and in the way he talked; it was there in the very sound of his voice, and his congregation sensed it, in the unthinking way that people do sense such things. Something was wrong with the man that the Holy Book could not put right. Gene Sherrin had little in the way of spiritual guidance to offer the people of Monkford, because he had little of the stuff for himself. He was an angry man. He was angry with the good people of Monkford and he was angry with himself; he was even angry with the good Lord and his Holy Book. But most of all, he was angry with the three desperadoes who'd ridden into his town that day and taken everything from him.

Chapter 13

Over six months had passed before the three desperadoes decided it was time to pay another visit on the good citizens of Monkford. They chose a Sunday to ride into town, as they had done last time.

They could hear the voices of the good folk that made up the congregation singing *Onward Christian Soldiers*, as they made their way along the main drag. They left their horses outside the church, then went inside. No sooner had they shown their faces than the singing faltered and then, within seconds, came to a complete stop.

'Why it's mighty kind of you folk,' Lee said in a voice that was loud enough for everyone to hear, 'to pay your respects by stoppin' your singin' like that. Now if you'll all kindly hand over your valuables to my two friends while they make their collection then I'd be most truly grateful. Gentlemen, we'll need your wallets. Ladies, you can speed things up by taking off your jewellery now, so you're ready to hand it all over. Sooner we get everythin' collected, sooner we can leave you good people in peace. And I'd like you all to know that you can rest assured our collection will go to a very good cause.'

Everyone started handing over their money and valuables, as Earl and Hank went round, and nobody said a word. Not until the Minister's voice rang out, loud and clear: 'That's enough! I will not suffer you to come into the good Lord's house like this and desecrate everything He stands for!'

Lee looked at the Minister and grinned. 'So just what do you plan to do about it, Minister?'

Gene Sherrin drew a pistol from his pocket. 'Turn round and get out of here now,' he said. 'I won't say it again.'

'That written somewhere in the Good Book, Minister?'

'Get out, you vermin!'

The grin left Lee's face, and he went for the gun in his holster; but Gene Sherrin fired first. The bullet hit Lee in the chest, and he froze a moment and then fell to the floor. The next moment, Earl drew and fired at the Gene Sherrin and got him in the gut. Gene felt like he'd been kicked in the belly by a horse, but even so he managed to fire a shot in return, and he hit Earl in the arm, so that Earl dropped his gun. Meanwhile, Hank had fired two shots at the Minister and missed both times. He fired again, and this time he got the Minister in the chest. The Minister staggered across the altar and fell to the ground, dead.

Seeing this, the men in the congregation seized Hank and Earl, before they could fire any more bullets, and they took their guns from them. Then they took the men out into the street, and lynched them, right there, outside the church.

About the Author

Nick's crime novel, *The Long Siesta* (Grey Cells Press, the crime imprint of Holland House, September, 2015), was praised by a number of top crime authors, including Nicholas Blincoe, Caro Ramsay, Paul Johnston and Howard Linskey. Critic Barry Forshaw also wrote a positive review of the novel in *Crime Time* and followed up by giving Nick and his book a mention in *Brit Noir*, a guide to the best contemporary British crime writing and film.

Nick has also had stories included in prestigious anthologies in recent months, including *The Mammoth Book of Jack The Ripper Stories* (Little Brown, ed. Maxim Jakubowski) and *Sunshine Noir*. Nick's first crime novel, *Flowers At Midnight*, was published by Moonshine Cove, an American publisher, in 2012, and it was praised by the likes of Vincent Lardo and Quentin Bates. He has had around twenty short stories published in North American magazines, including *Descant* and the *Evergreen Review*.

So far, Nick's books can be divided up into crime novels, like *Bad In Bardino*, and works which are centred more on relationships, such as *One Flesh* - which focuses on a love tangle set in a Welsh mining village in the 1980s. Another of Nick's novels, *Young Hearts*, tells the story of a love triangle set against the backdrop of World War One, while *One Flesh* concerns itself with gay as well as heterosexual love.

Nick's crime novels can also be divided into different sub-categories. For instance, *Bad In Bardino*, is a PI novel set in Spain, and in this book, which is told in the first person, we see everything through the private detective's eyes; while *Switch* and *Only The Lonely*, both set in London, are shorter but pacy stories in which we see the action from different points of view – often through the eyes of the criminals. With *The Long Siesta*, a third-person narrative set in Seville, Nick again chose to tell the story so that all of the action is seen through the eyes of the main character, in this case Spanish police detective Inspector Jefe Velázquez.

Nick is British, but is currently living with his family in Fuengirola, Spain. Originally from Bristol, he studied at the universities of Cardiff and London, and lived for a long time in the English capital, where he ended up teaching English Literature and English Language in an FE college. He has moved around a fair bit, and has also lived and taught in Saudi Arabia, Abu Dhabi, Brighton, Barcelona, Bilbao and the city of Malaga. His experience of life in different places has helped his writing, and his books are set against a range of backdrops.

Nick has always taken a keen interest in sport, particularly in cricket and football, and he was a useful cricketer in his youth, having opened the batting regularly for Downend's first eleven in the Western League.

Nick speaks Spanish fluently and reads widely in both English and Spanish. If he had to choose his all-time favourite crime novels, then *The Long Goodbye* and *The Postman Always Rings Twice* would both be up near the top of the list. Elmore Leonard's *Pronto*, *Get Shorty* or *Bandits* and Jim Thompson's *The Getaway* would also figure, as would Dashiell Hammett's *The Glass Key*. Nick also loves to read contemporary crime writers, to keep up with what his peers are doing, and is as likely to be found reading the latest Ian Rankin, Don Winslow or Lee Child, say, as rereading Tolstoy or Hemingway, or Don Quijote in the original Spanish.

Anyone who reads *One Flesh* and then goes on to read *Bad In Bardino* (or vice versa), might be excused for thinking these books must have been written by different authors, so different are they in terms not only of subject matter but also style. If so, then Nick would be happy with this state of affairs, because he feels that authors should try to keep their own personalities out of their books as far as possible.

Nick wants people to enjoy reading his books and keep turning the pages, and he would like to encourage satisfied readers to post reviews on Amazon or Goodreads, or wherever they see fit.

Lightning Source UK Ltd.
Milton Keynes UK
UKHW021845201120
373796UK00003B/481